Christ in the Fields

Eugene McCabe was born in Glasgow in 1930. His work includes *Heritage and Other Stories*, from which two of the stories in this trilogy have been taken: *Cancer* received the Writers' Award at Prague International in 1974. *Victims*, a short novel, won the Holtby Award from the Royal Society of Literature (1976). Eugene McCabe has also written a number of plays. He lives and works on a farm on the Monaghan/Fermanagh border.

Also by Eugene McCabe

Stage plays
King of the Castle
Breakdown
Pull Down a Horseman
Swift
Gale Day

Television plays
adapted from original prose works
A Matter of Conscience
Some Women on the Island
The Funeral
Cancer
Heritage
Siege
Roma
Music at Annahuillon

Prose
Heritage and other stories
Cyril (children's fable)
Death and Nightingales (novel)

CHRIST IN THE FIELDS

A Fermanagh Trilogy

EUGENE McCABE

Minerva

These three tales (published separately) were
conceived as one. This is their first time
to be published in one volume.

A Minerva Paperback
CHRIST IN THE FIELDS
A FERMANAGH TRILOGY

Cancer first published in *The Dublin Magazine*
Published in *Heritage and Other Stories*
by Victor Gollancz 1978
Heritage first published in
Heritage and Other Stories by Victor Gollancz 1978
Victims first published by Victor Gollancz 1976

This collection first published 1993 in Minerva
by Mandarin Paperbacks
Michelin House, 81 Fulham Road, London SW3 6RB

Minerva is an imprint of the Octopus Publishing Group,
a division of Reed International Books Limited

A CIP catalogue record for this book
is available from the British Library
ISBN 0 7493 9871 X

Printed and bound in Great Britain
by Cox and Wyman Ltd, Reading, Berks

Contents

For all who have suffered
through the old trouble,
this book is dedicated
both in sorrow and hope

Cancer

Today there was an old Anglia and five bicycles outside the cottage. Boyle parked near the bridge. As he locked the car Dinny came through a gap in the ditch: 'Busy?'

'From the back of Carn Rock and beyont: it's like a wake inside.'

For a living corpse Boyle thought.

'How is he?'

'Never better.'

'No pain?'

'Not a twitch . . . ates rings round me and snores the night long.' Boyle imagined Joady on the low stool by the hearth in the hot, crowded kitchen, his face like turf ash. Everyone knew he was dying. Women from townlands about had offered to cook and wash. Both brothers had refused. 'Odd wee men,' the women said. 'Course they'd have no sheets, and the blankets must be black.' 'And why not,' another said, 'no woman body ever stood in aither room this forty years.' At which another giggled and said, 'or lay'. And they all laughed because Dinny and Joady were under-sized. And then they were ashamed of laughing and said 'poor Joady cratur' and 'poor Dinny he'll be left: that's worse'. And people kept bringing things: bacon and chicken,

3

whiskey and stout, seed cake, fresh-laid eggs, wholemeal bread; Christmas in February.

In all his years Joady had never slept away from the cottage so that when people called now he talked about the hospital, the operation, the men who died in the ward. In particular he talked about the shattered bodies brought to the hospital morgue from the explosion near Trillick. When he went on about this, Protestant neighbours kept silent. Joady noticed and said: 'A bad doin', Albert, surely, there could be no luck after thon.' To Catholic neighbours he said: 'Done it their selves to throw blame on us' and spat in the fire.

It was growing dark at the bridge, crows winging over from Annahullion to roost in the fibrous trees about the disused Spade Mill.

'A week to the day we went up to Enniskillen,' Dinny said.

'That long.'

'A week to the day, you might say to the hour. Do you mind the helicopter?' He pointed up. 'It near sat on that tree.'

Boyle remembered very clearly. It had seemed to come from a quarry of whins, dropping as it crossed Gawley's flat. Like today he had driven across this border bridge and stopped at McMahon's iron-roofed cottage. Without looking up, he could sense the machine chopping its way up from the Spade Mill. He left the car engine running. Dinny came out clutching a bottle of something. The helicopter hung directly over a dead alder in a scrub of egg bushes between the cottage and the river. Dinny turned and flourished the bottle upwards shouting above the noise: 'I hope to Jasus yis are blown to shit.' He grinned and waved the bottle again. Boyle

4

looked up. Behind the curved, bullet-proof shield two pale urban faces stared down, impassive.

'Come on, Dinny, get in.'

He waved again: a bottle of Lucozade.

Boyle put the car in gear and drove North. They could hear the machine overhead. Dinny kept twisting about in the front seat trying to see up.

'The whores,' he screeched, 'they're trackin' us.'

On a long stretch of road the helicopter swooped ahead and dropped to within a yard of the road. It turned slowly and moved towards them, a gigantic insect with revolving swords. Five yards from the car it stopped. The two faces were now very clear: guns, uniform, apparatus, one man had ear-phones. He seemed to be reading in a notebook. He looked at the registration number of Boyle's car and said something. The helicopter tilted sharply and rose clapping its way towards Armagh across the sour divide of fields and crooked ditches. Boyle remained parked in the middle of the road, until he could hear nothing. His heart was pumping strongly: 'What the hell was all that?'

'They could see we had Catholic faces,' Dinny said and winked. There was a twist in his left eye. 'The mouth' McMahon neighbours called him, pike lips set in a bulbous face, a cap glued to his skull. Boyle opened a window. The fumes of porter were just stronger than the hum of turf smoke and a strong personal pong.

'It's on account of Trillick,' Boyle said, 'they'll be very active for a day or two.'

'You'll get the news now.'

Boyle switched on the car radio and a voice was saying: 'Five men in a Land Rover on a track leading to a television transmitter station on Brougher Mountain near Trillick between Enniskillen and Omagh. Two BBC officials and three workers lost their lives. An

Army spokesman said that the booby trap blew a six-foot deep crater in the mountainside and lifted the Land Rover twenty yards into a bog. The bodies of the five men were scattered over an area of 400 square yards. The area has been sealed off.'

Boyle switched off the radio and said: 'Dear God.'

The passed a barn-like church set in four acres of graveyard. Dinny tipped his cap to the dead; McCaffreys, Boyles, Grues, Gunns, McMahons, Courtneys, Mulligans; names and bones from a hundred townlands.

'I cut a bit out of the *Anglo-Celt* once,' Dinny said, 'about our crowd, the McMahons.'

'Yes?'

'Kings about Monaghan for near a thousand years, butchered, and driv' north to these bitter hills, that's what it said, and the scholar that wrote it up maintained you'll get better bred men in the cabins of Fermanagh than you'll find in many's a big house.'

Boyle thumbed up at the graveyard: 'One thing we're sure of, Dinny, we'll add our bit.'

'Blood tells,' Dinny said, 'it tells in the end.'

A few miles on they passed a waterworks. There was a soldier pacing the floodlit jetty.

'Wouldn't care for his job, he'll go up with it some night.'

'Unless there's changes,' Boyle said.

'Changes! What changes. Look in your neighbour's face; damn little change you'll see there. I wrought four days with Gilbert Wilson before Christmas, baggin' turf beyont Doon, and when the job was done we dropped into Corranny pub, and talked land, and benty turf, and the forestry takin' over and the way people are leavin' for factories, the pension scheme for hill farmers and a dose of things: no side in any of it, not one word of politics or religion, and then all of a shot he leans over to me and says: "Fact is, Dinny, the time I like you best, I could cut your throat." A quare slap in the mouth, but I didn't rise to it; I just said: "I'd as lief not hear the like, Gilbert." "You," says he, "and all your kind, it must be said." "It's a mistake, Gilbert, to say the like, or think it." "Truth," he said, "and you mind it, Dinny".'

He looked at Boyle: 'What do you think of that for a spake?'

They came to the main road and Moorlough: 'Are them geese or swans,' Dinny was pointing. He wound down his window and stared out. On the Loughside field there seemed to be fifty or sixty swans, very white against the black water. Boyle slowed for the trunk road, put on his headlights.

'Hard to say.'

'Swans,' Dinny said.

'You're sure?'

'Certain sure.'

'So far from water?'

'I seen it before on this very lake in the twenties, bad sign.'

'Of what?'

'Trouble.'

The lake was half a mile long and at the far end of it there was a military checkpoint. An officer came over with a boy soldier and said, 'Out, please.' Two other soldiers began searching the car.

'Name?'

'Boyle, James.'

'Occupation?'

'Teacher.'

'Address?'

'Tiernahinch, Kilrooskey, Fermanagh.'

'And this gentleman?'

7

Boyle looked away. Dinny said nothing. The officer said again: 'Name?'

'Denis McMahon, Gawley's Bridge, Fermanagh.'

'Occupation?'

'I'm on the national health.'

The boy beside the officer was writing in a notebook. A cold wind blowing from the lake chopped at the water, churning up angry flecks. The officer had no expression in his face. His voice seemed bored and flat.

'Going where?'

'Enniskillen,' Boyle said.

'Purpose?'

'To visit this man's brother, he's had an operation.'

'He's lying under a surgeont,' Dinny said.

The officer nodded.

'And your brother's name?'

'Joady, Joseph, I'm next-of-kin.'

The boy with the notebook went over to a radio jeep. The officer walked away a few paces. They watched. Boyle thought he should say aloud what they were all thinking, then decided not to; then heard himself say: 'Awful business at Trillick.'

The officer turned, looked at him steadily for a moment and nodded. There was another silence until Dinny said: 'Trillick is claner nor a man kicked to death by savages fornenst his childer.'

The officer did not look round. The boy soldier came back from the jeep and said everything was correct, Sir. The officer nodded again, walked away and stood looking at the lake.

Dinny dryspat towards the military back as they drove off. ' "And this gentleman!" Smart bugger, see the way he looked at me like I was sprung from a cage.'

'His job, Dinny!'

8

'To make you feel like an animal! "Occupation" is right!'

Near Lisnaskea Dinny said: 'Cancer, that's what we're all afraid of, one touch of it and you're a dead man. My auld fella died from a rare breed of it. If he went out in the light, the skin would rot from his face and hands, so he put in the latter end of his life in a dark room, or walkin' about the roads at night. In the end it killed him. He hadn't seen the sun for years.'

He lit a cigarette butt.

'A doctor tould me once it could be in the blood fifty years, and then all of a shot it boils up and you're a gonner.'

For miles after this they said nothing, then Dinny said: 'Lisbellaw for wappin' straw,/Maguiresbridge for brandy./Lisnaskea for drinkin' tay./But Clones town is dandy/ . . . that's a quare auld one?'

He winked with his good eye.

'You want a jigger, Dinny?'

'I'll not say no.'

Smoke, coughing, the reek of a diesel stove and porter met them with silence and watching. Dinny whispered: 'U.D.R., wrong shop.'

Twenty or more, a clutch of uniformed farmers, faces hardened by wind, rutted from bog, rock and rain, all staring, invincible, suspicious.

'Wrong shop,' Dinny whispered again.

'I know,' Boyle said, 'we can't leave now.'

Near a partition there was a space beside a big man. As Boyle moved towards it a woman bartender said: 'Yes?'

'Two halfs, please.'

'What kind?'

'Irish.'

'What kind of Irish?'

'Any kind.'

Big enough to pull a bullock from a shuck on his own Boyle thought as the big man spat at the doosy floor and turned away. Dinny nudged Boyle and winked up at a notice pinned to a pillar. Boyle read:

Linaskea and District Development Association
Extermination of Vermin
1/- for each magpie killed.
2/- for each grey crow killed.
10/- for each grey squirrel killed.
£1 for each fox killed.

Underneath someone had printed with a biro:

For every Fenian Fucker: one old penny.

As the woman measured the whiskies a glass smashed in the snug at the counter end. A voice jumped the frosted glass: 'Wilson was a fly boy, and this Heath man's no better, all them Tories is tricky whores, dale with Micks and Papes and lave us here to rot. Well, by Christ, they'll come no Pope to the townland of Invercloon, I'll not be blown up or burned out, I'll fight to the last ditch.'

All listening in the outer bar, faces, secret and serious, uncomfortable now as other voices joined: 'Your right, George.'

'Sit down, man, you'll toss the table.'

'Let him say out what's in his head.'

'They'll not blow me across no bog; if it's blood they want then, by Jasus, they'll get it, all they want, gallons of it, wagons, shiploads.'

'Now you're talking, George.'

The big man looked at the woman. She went to the

hatch, pushed it and said something into the snug. The loudness stopped. A red-axe face stared out, no focus in the eyes. Someone snapped the hatch shut. Silence. The big man spat again and Dinny said: 'I'd as lief drink with pigs.'

He held his glass of whiskey across the counter, poured it into the bar sink and walked out. Boyle finished his whiskey and followed.

In the car again, the words came jerking from Dinny's mouth: 'Choke and gut their own childer. Feed them to rats.'

He held up a black-rimmed nail to the windscreen.

'Before they'd give us *that*!'

'It's very sad,' Boyle said, 'I see no answer.'

'I know the answer, cut the bastards down, every last one of them and it'll come to that, them or us. They got it with guns, kep' it with guns, and guns'll put them from it.'

'Blood's not the way,' Boyle said.

'There's no other.'

At Eniskillen they went by the low end of the town, passed armoured cars, and the shattered Crown buildings. Outside the hospital there were four rows of cars, two police cars and a military lorry. Joady's ward was on the ground floor. He was in a corner near a window facing an old man with bad colour and a caved-in mouth. In over thirty years Boyle had never seen Joady without his cap. Sitting up now in bed like an old woman, with a white domed head and drained face, he looked like Dinny's ghost shaved and shrunk in regulation pyjamas. He shook hands with Boyle and pointed at Dinny's bottle: 'What's in that?'

'Lucozade,' Dinny said.

'Poison.'

'It's recommended for a sick body.'

'Rots the insides: you can drop it out the windy.'

'I'll keep it,' Dinny said, 'I can use it.'

Boyle could see that Dinny was offended, and remembered his aunt's anger one Christmas long ago. She had knit a pair of wool socks for Joady and asked him about them.

'Bad wool, Miss,' he said, 'out through the heel in a week, I dropped them in the fire.'

She was near tears as she told his mother: 'Ungrateful, lazy, spiteful little men, small wonder Protestants despise them and us, and the smell in that house . . . you'd think with nothing else to do but draw the dole and sit by the fire the least they could do is wash themselves: as for religion, no Mass, no altar, nothing ever, they'll burn, they really will, and someone should tell them. God knows you don't want thanks, but to have it flung back in your teeth like that it's . . . '

'It's very trying, Annie,' his mother said.

And Boyle wanted to say to his aunt: 'No light, no water, no work, no money, nothing all their days, but the dole, fire poking, neighbour baiting, and the odd skite on porter, retched off that night in a ditch.'

'Communists,' his aunt mocked Joady, 'I know what real Communists would do with those boyos, what Hitler did with the Jews.'

'Annie, that's an awful thing to say.'

There was silence and then his aunt said: 'God forgive me, it is, but . . . ' and then she wept.

'Because she never married, and the age she's at,' his mother said afterwards.

Joady was pointing across a square of winter lawn to the hospital entrance: 'Fornenst them cars,' he said, 'the morgue.' His eyes swivelled round the ward, 'I heard nurses talk about it in the corridor, brought them here in plastic bags from Trillick, laid them out on slabs in a go of sawdust on account of the blood. That's what they're at now, Army doctors tryin' to put the bits together, so's their people can recognise them, and box them proper.'

The old man opposite groaned and shifted. Joady's voice dropped still lower: 'They say one man's head couldn't be got high or low, they're still tramping the mountain with searchlights.'

'Dear God,' Boyle said.

'A fox could nip off with a man's head handy enough.'

'If it came down from a height it could bury itself in that auld spongy heather and they'd never find it or less they tripped over it.'

'Bloodhound dogs could smell it out.'

'They wouldn't use bloodhound dogs on a job like that, wouldn't be proper.'

'Better nor lavin' it to rot in a bog, course they'd use dogs, they'd have to.'

'Stop!'

Across the ward the old man was trying to elbow himself up. The air was wheezing in and out of his lungs, he seemed to be choking: 'Stop! Oh God, God, please, I must go . . . I must . . .'

Boyle stood up and pressed the bell near Joady's bed. Visitors round other beds stopped talking. The wheezing got louder, more irregular, and a voice said: 'Someone do something.'

Another said: 'Get a doctor.'

Boyle said: 'I've rung.'

A male nurse came and pulled a curtain round the bed. When a doctor came the man was dead. He was pushed away on a trolley covered with a white sheet. Gradually people round other beds began to talk. A young girl looking sick was led out by a woman.

'That's the third carted off since I come down here.'

'Who was he?' Boyle asked.

'John Willie Foster, a bread server from beyont Five-miletown, started in to wet the bed like a child over a year back, they couldn't care for him at home, so they put him to "Silver Springs", the auld people's home, but he got worse there so they packed him off here.'

'Age,' Dinny said, 'the heart gave up.'

'The heart broke,' Joady said, 'no one come to see him, bar one neighbour man. He was towld he could get home for a day or two at Christmas, no one come, he wouldn't spake with no one, couldn't quit' cryin'; the man's heart was broke.'

'Them Probsbyterians is a hard bunch, cauld, no nature.'

There was a silence.

'Did he say what about you Joady? . . . the surgeon?'

'No.'

'You asked?'

'"A deep operation," he said, "very deep, an obstruction," so I said "Is there somethin' rotten, Sir, I want to know, I want to be ready?" "Ready for what," says he and smiles, but you can't tell what's at the back of a smile like that. "Just ready," I said.

'"You could live longer nor me," says he.'

'He hasn't come next nor near me since I've come down here to the ground . . . did he tell yous anythin?'

'Dam' to the thing,' Dinny said.

And Boyle noticed that Joady's eyes were glassy.

There was a newspaper open on the bed. It showed the Duke of Kent beside an armoured car at a shattered customs post. On the top of the photograph the name of the post read 'Kilclean'. Boyle picked up the newspaper, opened it and saw headlines: 'Significance of bank raids'; 'Arms for Bogsiders'; 'Failure to track murderer'; 'Arms role of I.R.A.'

He read, skipping half, half listening to the brothers.

'In so far as ordinary secret service work is concerned, could be relied on and trusted . . . under the control of certain Ministers. Reliable personnel . . . co-operation between Army intelligence and civilian intelligence . . . no question of collusion.'

'Lies,' Joady said to Dinny, 'you don't know who to believe.' His voice was odd and his hand was trembling on the bedspread. Boyle didn't want to look at his face and thought, probably has it and knows. Dinny was looking at the floor.

'Lies,' Joady said again. And this time his voice sounded better. Boyle put down the paper and said: 'I hear you got blood, Joady.'

'Who towld you that?'

'One of my past pupils, a nurse here.'

'Three pints,' Joady said.

Boyle winked and said: 'Black blood, she told me you got Paisley's blood.'

Joady began shaking, his mouth opened and he seemed to be dry-retching. The laughter when it came was pitched and hoarse. He put a hand on his stitches and stopped, his breathing shallow, his head going like a picaninny on a mission box.

'Paisley's blood, she said that?'

'She did.'

'That's tarror,' he said, but was careful not to laugh again. Boyle stood up and squeezed his arm: 'We'll have to go, Joady, next time can we bring you something you need?'

'Nothin',' Joady said, 'I need nothin'.'

Walking the glass-walled, rubber corridor Boyle said: 'I'll wait in the car, Dinny.'

Dinny stopped and looked at the bottle of Lucozade: 'We could see him together.'

'If you want.'

The surgeon detached a sheet of paper from a file, he faced them across a steel-framed table: 'In your brother's case,' he was saying to Dinny, 'it's late, much, much, too late.' He paused, no one said anything and then the surgeon said: 'I'm afraid so.'

'Dying?'

'It's terminal.'

'He's not in pain,' Boyle said.

'And may have none for quite a while, when the stitches come out he'll be much better at home.'

'He doesn't know,' Dinny said.

'No, I didn't tell him yet.'

'He wants to know.'

The surgeon nodded and made a note on a sheet of paper. Dinny asked: 'How long has he got, Sir?'

The surgeon looked at the sheet of paper as though the death date were inscribed: 'Sometime this year . . . yes, I'm afraid so.'

The Anglia and bicycles were gone now. It had grown dark about the bridge and along the river. Boyle was cold sitting on the wall. Dinny had been talking for half an hour: 'He was never sick a day, and five times I've been opened, lay a full year with a bad lung above at Killadeas; he doesn't know what it is to be sick.'

Raucous crow noise carried up from the trees around the Spade Mill, cawing, cawing, cawing, blindflapping in the dark. They looked down, listening, waiting, it ceased. 'He knows about dying,' Boyle said.

'That's what I'm comin' at, he's dyin and sleeps twelve hours of the twenty-four, ates, smokes, walks, and for a man used never talk much, he talks the hind leg off a pot now, make your head light to hear him.'

He took out a glass phial: 'I take two of them sleeping

caps every night since he come home, and never close an eye. I can't keep nothin' on my stomach, and my skin itches all over; I sweat night and day. I'll tell you what I think: livin's worse nor dyin', and that's a fact.'

'It's upsetting, Dinny.'

It was dark in the kitchen: Joady gave Boyle a stool, accepted a cigarette, and lit it from the paraffin lamp, his face sharp and withered: a frosted crab.

'Where's the other fella gone?'

'I'm not sure,' Boyle said, 'he went down the river somewhere.'

Joady sucked on the cigarette: 'McCaffreys, he's gone to McCaffreys, very neighbourly these times, he'll be there until twelve or after.'

He thrust at a blazing sod with a one-pronged pitch fork: 'Same every night since I come home, away from the house every chance he gets.'

'All the visitors you have, Joady, and he's worried.'

'Dam' the worry, whingin' and whinin', to every slob that passes the road about *me* snorin' the night long, didn't I hear him with my own ears . . .'

He spat, his eyes twisting: 'It's *him* that snores not *me*, him: it's *me* that's dyin', *me*, not him . . . Christ's sake . . . couldn't he take a back sate until I'm buried.'

He got up and looked out the small back window at the night, at nothing: 'What would you call it, when your own brother goes contrary, and the ground hungry for you . . . eh! Rotten, that's what I'd call it, rotten.'

Heritage

He stepped back as the pigeon shattered through the dairy window. For an instant he saw the brown outstretched wings of the hawk, the yellow flouted eyes. It swerved sharply left with a screech, cutting under the archway, up over the beech copse in line with the orchard towards the border river. He was holding the dead pigeon as his mother and Maggie Reilly crossed from the porch, his mother's mouth a question mark, Maggie's face fat, flat and curious.

'There was a hawk after it,' he said.

'God help it,' his mother said with pitying eyes.

He left it on the dairy window.

'God made it.'

'Poor hunted cratur,' Maggie said.

His mother touched the plumage. 'These days every sound fright's me.'

She had a grey dress on for service. Maggie had green Sunday buttons sewn on her Monday coat, a floppy brown woollen that covered her fourteen stone.

'I'll have your milk in ten minutes Maggie, I've cans to collect.'

'No hurry, Eric.'

Blister, his father's mongrel hound appeared from

somewhere and ran from the yard, the pigeon in its mouth.

'Nature's cruel too,' Maggie said.

Eric watched them walk towards the house. Maggie had two children by different men, and lived in the office section of a disused creamery.

'A proper Papist hedge whore,' George said often to his mother. 'You should get shut of her, Sarah.'

'Indeed I should,' his mother said.

Maggie worked at other farms and helped out odd times with house parties at Inver Hall. Apart from harmless news his mother liked to hear, she was a good worker and likeable.

He went out under the stone archway. The rutted laneway, dry now in summer, had a thick tuft of scutch down its spine. On a stricken ash in the middle of the orchard the hawk perched in rigid silence. Eric stood and looked. It stared back sullen. He clapped his hands sharply. It fell from the branch, swooped across the lane, upwards from the rolling fields and stout ditches of Drumhowl.

He followed its flight towards Shannock and Carn Rock, a dim, hidden country, crooked scrub ditches of whin and thorns stunted in sour putty land; bare, spade-ribbed fields, rusted tin roofed cabins, housing a stony faced people living from rangy cattle and Welfare handouts. From their gaunt lands they looked down on the green border country below watching, waiting. To them a hundred years was yesterday, two hundred the day before.

'A rotten race,' George said, 'good for nothin' but malice and murder; the like of Hitler would put them through a burnhouse and spread them on their sour bogs and he'd be right, it's all they're fit for.'

The lane sloped steeply to the county road. He walked

by the orchard and beech copse planted by his grandfather in 1921 to block off the view of the Fenian South.
He could see through the grey-lichened trunks the slate
coloured river winding through thick rushy bottoms
past Inver Hall and Church towards Lough Erne. A
week ago he had watched a gun fight between British
soldiers and gunmen across the river in the Republic.
He saw one gunman hit and dragged away by two
others. His mouth was dry for hours after. Every other
day this last few years their windows rattled from
explosions in nearby towns and villages. Now since he
had joined the U.D.R. the thing had got ugly. Three
men he knew were dead, two U.D.R., one Catholic
policeman. To-night when he put on his uniform his
mother would be near tears. Every day when they talked
about land, neighbours or cattle prices, they were thinking something else. He was a big target. He could be
got handy. Death spitting from a gap or bog, a sharp
bend in the road, a cattle mart or shop counter, a booby
trapped pad between townlands, or blown asunder on
the tractor drawing turf from Doon forest, where it
seemed dark now in July. Anywhere, anytime, a clash
to the head or body, brain shattered, his name in a
news-reader's mouth:

'This evening in South Fermanagh, Eric O'Neill,
twenty-one, a part time member of the U.D.R.'

Where and how it happened, along with oil shortages,
strikes and rumours of revolution. T.V. coverage, a vast
Protestant attendance. The *Impartial Reporter* would
give it two full pages with photographs, his father,
George, Sam and Joe Robinson carrying the coffin, his
mother supported by neighbours at the graveside. More

hatred but he'd be gone from it. Forgot in a week except for Rachel and the family.

As he approached the milk stand he could see a label tied to the can handle. A reject? Then he noticed the envelope, black edged. Inside printed with red marker pen he read:

ERIC O'NEILL U.D.R. DRUMHOWL
BORN 1952
DIED ?
GET OUT . . . OR BE GOT LIKE CROZIER
R.I.P.

He felt more anger than fear. Even now as he stood they could be watching ten fields away or further, in a hedge, up a tree. He put the note in his pocket, grasped the churns, jumped the low ditch and walked up the back of the hedge, keeping out of sight of the road, through the orchard into the yard. He brought the cans straight to the dairy. As he loosened the lids to let air circulate, he noticed his hands were shaking like an old man's. He was sweating. 'I'm a coward,' he thought. He took out the note and read it again. 'R.I.P.' A sick, cruel touch that. One by one he thought of his Catholic neighbours from Drumhowl to Carn Rock, tried to imagine them writing this . . . all hard working people. Martin Cassidy the only active man in politics, a Civil Rights man; open and manly, respected by both sides.

Maggie came across the yard pushing her bicycle, a milk-can in one hand for two pints of milk, part payment for the work she did. She followed him into the byre.

'You tend them well, Eric, great cows God bless them.'

She said this every day, or something like it. She

understood the work that went into the feeding, cleaning and milking of twenty-three cows, the awkward calvings, calf scours, sudden deaths. She looked at him now with clear kind eyes, but of another race and creed, who might by now have decided on the time and place of his death. Eric hunkered to attach a milk cluster.

'You can't tell what they're thinking,' George said 'never, ever.'

Straightening, he looked down at the four claws of the machine, the milk pulsing into the bucket.

'You're not talking to the people this morning, Eric.'

'Sorry, Maggie.'

He looked round. It was almost as if she knew. When she dropped her voice he listened carefully, looking straight into her eyes.

'Something to tell you, Eric,' she was saying.

'Yes?'

'A neighbour man.' She stopped and looked at the bright cobbled yard.

'This neighbour man, he told me he heard three men in a pub in Arva.'

'Yes?'

'Talkin' quiet. They had a list of names at a table.'

Colour had come into her face. She was finding this hard to say. He looked away, Maggie went on:

'From where he stood this neighbour man, he saw your name.'

'What sort of list?'

'I don't know . . . he said they were young men, not country boys.'

She stopped again. 'Could be another Eric O'Neill.'

'Me all right . . . maybe your neighbour left this for me.'

As she read the note her eyes filled, Eric watched. 'What neighbour man, Maggie?'

'A good man, wouldn't say a cross word to a dog.'

'Would he know the men with the list?'

'Never seen them in his life . . . he said they sounded like Tyrone.'

'The publican must know them?'

'I wouldn't know that, son.'

'How do they get names? How do they know when I come and go?'

He could hear a sharpness in his voice. She was staring with dilated eyes.

'They'll shoot postmen next.'

'Get out, son.'

'Maggie, I was in uniform, that's enough.'

He had known her since he was a child and had never seen her look frightened. She knew a man who knew men who carried guns and were prepared to kill. He was on their list and she had warned.

'I'd as lief die myself, Eric, as see you harmed.'

'I know that, Maggie.'

'Honest to God, I . . . '

'My worry, not yours . . . it's a bloody mess.'

Outside under the winch-gibbet on the byre gable he tapped two pints of milk from the cooler.

'What'll you do, son?'

She didn't hear him say 'I'm still alive' because of their old Bedford revving in the lane as it approached the arched entry. He watched it bounce over the stone gulley into the sunlit yard. His father reversed into the open turf-shed, cut the engine and opened a newspaper. Before he could think to stop her Maggie was moving towards the van. She talked with his father through the side window. When she left, his father got out of the van. He stood looking towards the byre, then walked towards the back porch of the house. One way or another they'd have heard. Notes like this had to be

26

shown to Dixon the Commandant; sooner or later they'd all know. Twenty-five U.D.R. men shot since he had joined, buried in parish graveyards, skulls and bodies smashed, married or single, in or out of uniform. He felt again a hatred for these hidden killers, the hatred he felt for rats; everywhere watching, waiting, in walls and ditches, dung heaps and gullies, following old ruts and runs, half blind, grubbing on filth, smelling out the weak, the crippled and the cowardly. Trap, cage, shoot, or poison, hunt them with terriers, ferrets or starving cats, and a month later they were back, scraping, clawing, gorging, no ridding the world of them.

'Thinking like George now,' he thought. 'Beginning to hate them, *all* of them.' Maggie? Sam's wife Maisie?

He tried not to think, finished the milking and crossed to the house. Pulling off his rubber boots in the glass porch he could see the kitchen door slightly open, voices loud inside; his mother's shrill. Silence for a few seconds. He pushed the hall door open a little. Sunlight from the kitchen window on the freshly polished linoleum, hand-made rugs, two stiff chairs and a hallstand, photographs of his O'Neill grandparents, an embroidered sampler, and a mahogany wall clock above the wainscotting.

'You pushed him in, woman, get him out now.'

'Cruel to say the like of that.'

'True: a death warrant, and you might as well have signed it, you and your brother George.'

His father's voice was quiet. It seldom changed tone. His mother said: 'He asked to join.'

'Made to feel a coward if he didn't; a gun, a uniform and the money's good, that's what you said . . . what he's got for himself won't bury him. Half his pay it took to put lino on that hall.'

'He gave that to me.'

27

'And you look down on Maggie Reilly.'

'You talk to me of her.'

'She loves her bastard sons, you've driv one away, and set the other up for a cock-shot . . . my sons.'

In the silence that followed Eric could feel his heart knocking strongly at his ribcage.

'It's me you hate, you've hated me for years.'

'I'd rather be dead than talk like this.'

'Better dead, a coward like all your people.'

When he heard his mother cry he pulled on his rubber boots, went out to the yard and stood at the gable of the house. Worse than fear, hearing them like that. The voices had stopped.

'Get out,' Sam said when he was leaving four years back.

'It's home,' Eric remembered saying.

Sam said, 'This place! It's a prison, worse; no drink, no smoke, no dance, no love, nothing but work, work, work and the Rev. Plumm every Sunday. Trouble or no trouble, no man could live in this house and stay sane.'

He heard the porch door open, saw his father cross the yard.

'Eric.'

He moved from the gable. 'Here.'

His father moved to join him; taller, leaner, a lined face under a weathered hat, deepset eyes, a huntsman, farmer and tradesman who could read the time on the Post Office clock from the far end of the street in Fivemiletown. He looked now at Eric very directly.

'Maggie told me.'

'Aye.'

'Your mother knows.'

'She'd have heard.'

'She'll go off her head.'

'Been off it since Sam married and before.'

28

Eric looked away, his father said: 'You could leave till things quieten.'

'In a hundred years? I'd as lief take my chance.'

'You'll be got if you stay.'

'Someone has to . . .'

'I don't want to bury you, son.'

'Someone must fight.'

'Who? Every second neighbour? American money? Gangs of street savages. There's a reason for all that and they can't all be locked up hung or shot, they'll come again, and again, and again 'till they get what they want, or most of it, the same the world over.'

Eric was tempted to say 'Like rats' but didn't.

'I should have stood my ground that night, put George out and sent her to bed and said No. I should have took a stand. Show us the note.'

He watched his father read. Two days of stubble seemed greyer.

'The whole thing makes me sick.'

He handed back the note: 'We'd best go in.'

At the table his mother sat, hair knotted up, scared eyes, her face white as eggshell. When Eric looked up she was staring straight at him, porridge and wheaten bread on the deal boards, silence but for the wall clock in the hall. Then his mother said:

'You blame me both of you.'

Eric said: 'I blame no one.'

'Whispering outside.'

'Talking,' his father said, 'we'll say it again if you want.'

'Men tortured in back streets, butchered fornenst their wives and childer, all of us awake when a car stops at night or the dog barks, and you blame me 'cause you think someone should take a stand.'

'What's he fighting for, woman, God and country?

The Queen? I'll tell you what he's fighting for . . . the big boys who splash more on week-ends whoring than he'll make in a lifetime, and good luck to their whoring I say, if there's goms who'll die to keep them at it; that's your cause, son, the one true God, pound notes, millions of them, and the men who have them don't care a tinker's curse who kills who as long as they keep their grip, and if that's a coward's talk, I'll stay one.'

'That's something you read in your trashy paper.'

'It's the truth, woman.'

'From a liar . . . and a hypocrite.'

'Take care.'

'You'll take what you get from Papist or Protestant . . . you don't care, and never will . . . tip your cap to money like anyone else and I'll not hear speeches 'bout big men and their rotten lives, when there's little men twice as rotten.'

'Like George?'

'He's not cruel to his own kin . . . you said things to me just now, John Willie, no man who calls himself a man should say to any woman, let alone his wife, things I'll not forget the longest day I live.'

His father was looking fixedly at a point on the kitchen floor, his face rigid. He said quiet and cold:

'You'll live to know worse days, woman.'

'God forgive you.'

'And you.'

She was beginning to break. 'The child is frightened.'

'I'm no child, Mother.'

'You didn't know what you were doing.'

His father said blunt. 'You did, George did. He signed, took the oath, money, what odds who's wrong or right, we've been over this a hundred times.'

'You don't care.'

'If one neighbour in ten thousand wants to kill me or

30

mine, I'll not hate them all for that one, and I don't hate someone I've never met.'

'Please, Da.'

'Maisie, your own daughter-in-law.'

'Please.'

He understood what his father was saying, he knew what his mother was feeling.

'You don't know right from wrong, woman, good from bad.'

'You're one to talk.'

'Say what you like to your brother and his Christian friends, I'll not hear it in my house.'

'A sad day I ever stood inside it.'

'Damn little you've ever done in it, but gripe and whine.'

She left the table stumbling as she went up the stairs, her bowl of porridge untouched. When they heard the bedroom door close, his father said:

'Day's I'd pay to be shot by anyone, dead and done with this crabbed life.'

'You shouldn't, Da.'

'What?'

'Talk so hard.'

'I have reason . . . take a drink, crack a joke and it's the end of the world, never heard her laugh right in thirty years, and never seen her body and won't or less she dies first and I'm at the laying out.'

'Don't.'

'True . . . I had land, a stone built house, after you two were born she'd all she wanted from me . . . hates bodies, her own and mine . . . even food, hates that, won't eat fornenst strange eyes . . . the other end of stooping, and that's shameful. She could live on black bread, water, the Bible and hating Catholics; that's enough to keep her happy, makes me sick. If I could

31

pray to God odd times it's not her blind God or George's. He's got a lot to answer for.'

Eric could not eat. His father did not look up when he said:

'I'll change.'

Passing his mother's room he could hear crying. He knocked.

'Yes.'

'Me.' He went in.

'Close the door, son.' Eric did as he was told.

'The cruel things that man says to me with his quiet voice. I'd as lief he'd shout or hit me.'

'We all say hard things be times.'

'He meant every word, God in Heaven, how could he say such things, let alone think them. I told Sam before he married her I wouldn't meet that girl or let her cross the door. I won't pretend about Papists, he hates me 'cause I tell the truth, he's afraid of that.'

Eric had heard this so often it was difficult for him to reply. If he disagreed she wept; if he seemed to agree even by silence she used this against his father . . . 'Eric agrees with me.'

'Am I speaking the truth, son, answer me?'

He picked his words carefully. 'You believe what you say is true, Mother.'

'I tell no lies.'

'I know.'

'Say what's in your head.'

'You're distressed, that bothers me more nor the note I got.'

She kissed his hand. 'I'll die if anything happens to you, Eric, and he'll blame me, we should leave, all of us.'

'How?'

'Just go.'

'Where?'

'Away from here, anywhere, if we go he'll have to go.'

'Sell out?'

'Yes.'

'He won't.'

'You were whispering out in the yard.'

'Mother, I'll go if you want but . . . '

'If you go, we all go, for good. I'll not stay and hear a son of mine called 'coward'. God I hate this house, these blind bitter fields.'

'We'll talk again.'

He kissed her forehead, went to his room and changed. When he came down to the kitchen his father was staring out of the window, the *Sunday People* open on the table. He picked up the paper and nodded at the door. As they crossed the yard his father asked:

'What's she on about?'

'The same.'

'Maisie?'

As they neared the turf shed the bedroom window went up with a snap. They stopped. Eric turned.

'Say it loud, John Willie.'

His father kept his back to the house.

'You'll die, man, I'll die, and the only son we can call our own will be murdered if we don't go!'

His father turned and said looking at the ground: 'If you want to go, woman, go, I'm staying.'

'And do what, man?'

'What you want.'

'Cook and scrub, is it? Wash and scald? I worked all my days for you, for next nothin' and when I ask one thing for myself, for your son, you say "no".'

'You've got *two* sons.'

His father dropped his voice and asked Eric: 'You want me to sell or go?'

'No.'

'Don't whisper,' his mother screamed, 'talk loud.'

'All right I'll talk loud . . . I was born here, I'll die here.'

'Keep your fifty rotten acres, bury yourself in them and your son, and don't blame me.'

Then the squeal of the window pulleys as the window snapped shut. Father and son stood in the sunlit yard looking at the ground.

'One thing to be said for the grave, you lie on your lone in a box; small wonder men die young, it's a wonder to Christ more don't hang themselves or walk out. What'll she pray about this morning in Church eh? "Love thy neighbour" is it?'

Blister came bounding round the side of the barn. John Willie opened the door of the old Bedford. The mongrel jumped into the back.

'I'm taking the van,' he said. 'You'll have to walk.'

Eric went back through the glass porch and stood listening in the long narrow hall. The wall clock, a tap turned in the bathroom, a helicopter somewhere far north. There was a smell of polish and paraffin oil. He opened the front door. July sunlight and the rich odour of cut grass. He looked at his pocketwatch, went back to the hallstand and took two hymnals.

'Mother.'

'Yes.'

'The van's gone.'

'I heard, what's the time?'

'Quarter to.'

Waiting at the hallstand he read the glazed and framed sampler stitched by his mother in memory of her own mother.

34

FOR ABIGAIL HAWTHORNE. 1874–1938
STRENGTH AND BEAUTY ARE HER CLOTH-
ING AND SHE SHALL LAUGH IN THE
LATTER DAY. THE LAW OF CLEMENCY
IS ON HER TONGUE. HER CHILDREN
HAVE RISEN UP AND CALLED HER BLESSED
... HER HUSBAND AND THEY HAVE
PRAISED HER. FAVOUR IS DECEITFUL AND
BEAUTY VAIN. THE WOMAN THAT
FEARETH THE LORD? SHE SHALL BE
PRAISED

Between a sundial and a floral corner her signature stitched over in black thread:

Sarah Hawthorne
October 1941

She came round the bend of the staircase white with
anger in her good Sunday coat and hat.

'Away with his filthy paper. Hunt ... and stupid beer
talk, anything but Church ... Where's he gone?'

'He didn't say.'

'Some Papist hovel up by Carn, thinks they like him,
'cause he can patch their slates and fix guttering, they'd
knife him quick as they'd look at him, he'll find that
out yet.'

She was so angry, so used to Eric's silence that they
walked by a farm pass to the back of Inver Church,
without exchanging another word. Eric was grateful for
the silence. July meadows baled or ensiled, pale or dark
green, uncut meadows on rising land a light fawn colour,
cows and dry stock content on good pasture. Over by
Cavan and the Cuilca Mountains the sky was a darkish

blue, but clear over the rock. It would be a good bright windy day.

Inver Church came into view as they topped a low drumlin, a small Romanesque block all spikes and parapets with one sharp spire to the front in two acres of burial ground, the family church of the Armstrongs, their mausoleum massive and dominating amongst plain weathered stones. Here his O'Neill grandparents were buried in the unkept grave. The Hawthornes' grave, his mother's people, had heavy protective railings around it forged by George. Even now in summer George kept it trim and neat with hedge clippers, particular, like his sister, to show evidence of Protestant order and privacy. He was waiting now at the stile in a dark suit topped by a white face and grey hair, uneasy, his head at an angle, a restive scaldcrow.

'Well?'

It was a rebuke and a question. Sarah answered: 'He took the van.'

George shrugged and sucked at his teeth: 'How's Eric?'

'Alive, George.'

His uncle's limestone eyes stared from under shag-black eyebrows, both stood aside to let his mother through the stile. George followed listening as his mother told about the note Eric dropped back. Twice George looked around with bleak concern. He tended the collection plate: there would be no time for talking until after the service. They went up the left aisle and sat in a pew near the baptistry under a white marble plaque, shaped like a shield. At the eagle lectern the Rev. John Plumm was reading from the Bible:

'And there is no remembrance now of former things nor indeed of those things which hereafter are to come.'

He paused and looked down at the half-full Church.

'All things in this time are mingled together, blood theft, murder, dissimulation, corruption and unfaithfulness, and men keep watches of madness in the night.'

In front of the lectern on the outside of the front pew sat Colonel Norbert Armstrong, erect and grey alongside his wife. Behind him a fine-skinned American with steel-rimmed glasses wearing a Norfolk jacket. Both pews were filled with the house party from Inver Hall. His father said often:

'They go for curiosity, to hear ould Plumm rave on, they believe in nothin' but land, stocks and shares, and keepin' things the way they are.'

Years ago he said he had seen a party of them bathing nude by moonlight in the shallow artificial lake fed from the border river. 'Blind drunk,' he said, 'leppin' on each other, men and women, squealing like cut pigs, a wonder to God the half of them weren't drowned.'

A week ago some Fenian wag hung a dated tourist poster on the main gates:

COME TO ULSTER FOR
YOUR SHOOTING HOLIDAYS

and smeared across it in green paint:

UP THE PROVOS

There was a rumour once that the Colonel had interfered with the game-keeper's son, and squashed a case with money. His father half believed the rumour, his mother rejected it as:

'Foul Papist lies. It's what they want to believe about all our kind.'

Every now and then the Colonel fired off letters to the *Irish Times* and the *Belfast Telegraph* about Law,

37

Order, Violence and the lunacy of Paisleyism. George bought the *Protestant Telegraph* and liked Paisley.

'The I.R.A. wouldn't waste a bullet on the Colonel,' he said once, but he tipped his cap as reverently as the next, and shod their hunters when requested at the Estate forge. The Rev. Plumm looked at the empty gallery on either side:

'If thou shall see the oppression of the poor, and violent judgements, and justice prevented in the province, wonder not at this matter, for he that is high hath another higher, and there are others still higher than these.' Eric watched George across the aisle, a daw listening for worms.

'All human things are liable to perpetual change. We are to rest on God's providence and cast away fruitless cares. I said in my heart concerning the sons of men, that God would prove them, and show them to be like beasts. Therefore the death of man, and of beasts is one; and the conditions of them both is equal; as man dieth, so they also die, all things breathe alike; and man hath nothing more than beast; all things are subject to vanity. And all things go to one place; of earth they are made and into earth they return together.'

The Rev. Plumm turned from the lectern. George got up and moved for the collection plate. All stood to sing, Miss Pritchard fingering the introductory phrases of Psalm three:

> Oh Lord, how are my foes increased!
> Against me many rise.
> Many say of my soul, for him
> In God no succour lies
> Yet thou my shield and glory art,
> The uplifter of mine head.
> I cried and from His Holy hill

The Lord me answer made,
I laid me down and slept, I waked;
For God sustained me
I will not fear though thousands ten
Set round against me be
Arise, O Lord; Save me, my God
For Thou has struck my foes
Upon the cheek; the wicked's teeth
Hast broken by Thy blows
Salvation surely doth belong
Unto the Lord alone;
Thy blessing, Lord, for ever more
Thy people is upon.

Service over, the Rev. Plumm walked into the presbytery. The Colonel stood in the aisle to allow his guests out first, English mostly, Eric thought, over with a pack of otter hounds he had seen yesterday from the haggard, a mahogany trailer towed by a yellow Land Rover. When the house party had filed out the Colonel walked down the aisle glancing and nodding here and there. Tom and Ruth Robinson followed with Joe and the rest of the congregation. Rachel remained seated. Eric smiled at Tom Robinson, an arthritic old farmer with a strong face. He winked at Joe who scarcely nodded back. When the church was empty Rachel looked around. Eric went into the baptistry; she followed. Through the high Gothic window they could see the sunlit graveyard, George and his mother talking with Rachel's parents, Joe sitting by himself on a tomb slab smoking a cigarette. A fine boned narrow face like Rachel's, which seldom showed colour or emotion, the same cool eyes, hair like bleached deal, Joe's ruffled at the nape, his skin coarsened by work and weather. Miss Pritchard was playing something complicated. It was hard to talk with the sound of the organ. Rachel took his hand and said:

'I've got 'till tomorrow, night duty next week. Were you talking to Joe?'

'He looked worried.'

She hesitated. 'Last night they stopped me near Maguiresbridge, three of them in tunics and berets.'

She was looking out at the graveyard.

'When they found I was Joe Robinson's sister one of them said "We should eff her arseways, only she might like it", another showed me a pistol and said "See this you black bitch, I'll ram it between your legs next time you, your brother or any of his like puts a hand on any of ours, and tell him from us we'll blow his effing brains out first chance we get".'

The words, and the quiet way she told it startled him more than if it had been screamed. The note in his pocket now seemed trivial; he could feel blood coming into his face. He said:

'They mean it.'

'I know. I begged Joe all night to get out, he won't listen, will you talk to him, Eric?'

He shrugged.

'You can try.'

'Your auld fellow's not fit to work, your place'd go to rack without Joe, even if he did get out what would he do? Where would he go?'

'Dig tunnels in Britain, anything; at least we could sleep at night.'

'I'm not leaving, and I got a note tied to a can this morning.'

'A note?'

'A warning.'

'From them?'

'Who else?'

40

'Oh God.'

The organ was pumping so loudly they were almost lip-reading. They waited for the passage of music to stop. On the baptistry wall on a large sheet of rectangular bronze, there was an engraved account of the Armstrong family, their arrival with King William, battles, sieges, glory, death and reference to the 'disaffected Irish'. In this marble font under this window both had been baptised in Christ to serve God and love neighbours. All round the church walls heraldic inscriptions, faded flags, sculptured guns, flutes, pipes, bayonets and loving tributes to violent death in Gallipoli, Flanders, Germany, North Africa.

'Catholics kneel under plaster saints,' his father remarked once, 'we sit with Christ under guns and swords.'

The Rev. Plumm came down the aisle dispensing a nod towards the baptistry.

'Why do we come here?'

'It marks the week.'

When the Rev. Plumm was gone Rachel said: 'Let's go out.'

From the arched entrance they saw groups of neighbours standing about exchanging news and views, George mouthing strongly with his mother and the Robinsons, an old forge bellows, the hiss of iron in the cooling tub. As Rachel moved into the sunlight to join them, Eric said:

'I want a word with Joe.'

He went over, handed him the note, and said: 'Rachel told me about last night.'

Joe read the note and handed it back without a word. He was looking across the river at the lime-washed Catholic church half a mile away, a plain stucco barnlike building, with a separate belfry, a white Madonna in a cave between the church and the curate's bungalow, a full congregation funnelling through the square porch spreading through their graveyard.

'Bees from a hive,' Eric said.

'Wasps,' Joe said.

'Any notion who stopped her?'

Joe shook his head.

'All Fenians round here, could be any of them.'

'You believe that?'

'What odds what I believe or you . . . they'll choose the time and place, pick us off, no chance to fight back.'

'Unless we go.'

'I can't.'

'Nor me.'

'Do your people know?'

'What?'

'About last night; Rachel?'

Joe shook his head. 'They're worried enough.'

Cars were beginning to move from the Catholic church park down to the border bridge, the sun throwing flashes of hostile light from windscreens as they turned up for Carn. Joe jerked his head towards the gaunt uplands.

'It's a jungle from here to the rock; they don't need phones, radios or helicopters; sneeze at the back of a ditch, they know who it was and why he was there; they know every move, we don't stand a chance.'

True. It was what Eric had told Maggie two hours ago. A lot of men got notes and were still alive. There was no point in further talk. Eric asked:

'You goin' to the hunt?'

'What hunt?'

'Otter, some pack from across, come last night to the Inver crowd. My auld fella's goin'.'

42

'In our house they're death on doing anything of a Sunday.'

'So's my mother and George, we might as well walk after dogs as sit and worry.'

'What time?'

'Three, at the Hall.'

'I'll come if I can.'

'Bring Rachel.'

'She hates huntin'.'

'Ask her anyway.'

Eric went over to join the others. Old Tom Robinson was looking at the gravel, squat in his late sixties, his wife Ruth, a tall thin woman with a forlorn face, blinking against the light, watching Eric approach. His mother was touching her upper lip nervously, upset by what George was saying. Eric heard him rasp:

'If we don't do it to them, they'll do it to us, and that's the story to the bitter end.'

Old Tom looked embarrassed. George looked at Eric: 'Any man tries to slide out is no man.'

I'm not sliding out George.'

His mother said: 'He's not your son, George . . . '

'More to me nor his own father. When it comes to the bit I can depend on him.'

Old Tom said, 'I'll run you up, Sarah.'

'It's only ten minutes,' his mother protested.

'Take the lift, mam,' Eric said. 'I'll walk.'

He nodded at the Robinsons and Rachel and moved away.

George called, 'Hould on, son, hould on.'

Eric slowed, waiting.

'What's your hurry?'

Eric was tempted to say, 'I don't want to listen to you George.' He said nothing. Afraid of George, of his mother, afraid to pick between his mother and his father, afraid of Catholics, afraid to hate or love. It was from George as a child that he first heard about Catholics in the forge at Oakfield:

'I'll shoe no Catholic ass, my boot in his hole.'

And some of the Protestant men in the forge took out their pipes and laughed. Others said: 'You're an awful man, George.'

But even as a child he knew they agreed with George. When a Catholic did bring work he was greeted with 'Well?' or 'What's wrong now?' or 'What are you trickin' at this weather?' With Protestant neighbours he was courteous and helpful. 'How's all the care, Bob?' No Catholics had come near his forge now for three years. He jerked his head towards the lime-washed church across the river.

'I'll say one thing for them, they're animals with balls, our side whines like Ruth Robinson . . . what's the end of it to be at all, at all, at all. Whiners get their teeth kicked down their throats.'

George slashed at a nettle on a neglected grave with his blackthorn.

'Have you lost your tongue?'

'You have all the questions and answers, George.'

'I know my mind, son, and you know yours if you were let, your father doesn't give a damn, and your mother wants you out, am I right?'

'Out where? I took an oath George, I'll stick by it.'

'Now you're talkin'.'

From the stile, across a narrow humped field of thistle and ragwort lay George's forge, a low squat crypt separate from the slated house, three fine oak trees at the back, proof to passing poverty in second hand cars that Oakfield could grow sound hardwood.

'Come on up a while, we'll brew tay and talk.'

Eric wanted to refuse but had no ready excuse. He

nodded assent. Every day of childhood, summer and winter, on his way home from school he had called with George, running messages across the spongy river bottoms to Johnson's border shop, black green rushes so high he sometimes lost his way, always a reward for his trouble, a slice of bread and butter sprinkled with caster sugar. In this world of small fields and bogland he had loved and still did, this coarse bigoted man with his rasping voice. No matter how he spewed blind hatred, it was difficult to disengage from the past, to scrap old memories. The lane they walked on now was rutted by a thousand carts, the bramble shoots reaching half-way across as they did every summer.

'A good straight man,' his mother said. 'The best blacksmith in Ulster, afraid of nothing and no one.'

'You're wrong,' his father said, 'he's afeered of everyone and everything, drinks every penny he gets and too mean to marry, and all that loud rough talk; thinks he hates Catholics, it's himself he hates, and I wouldn't fault him for that.'

In the sepia light of the kitchen George wet strong tea from the black range. They faced each other across the blue checkered oil-cloth; on the wall smokey portraits of the Queen, Carson and Paisley, a row of faded sashes, a large drum sitting beside a disused dash-churn in one corner, alongside it a thick pile of *Protestant Telegraphs*. As a child the sound of the drum frightened Eric so much that he crept to his mother's bed at night.

'It's only uncle George with his drum,' she whispered, 'nothin' to be afeered of.'

This last few nights ten townlands could hear him thumping at the dusk beside the iron scrap heap behind the forge. Next Thursday on the Twelfth at Fivemiletown, he would make it reverberate to the whole mountain. He took a sip of tea now from his mug and stared out the window, a welt on his left cheek where a mare had lashed it twenty years ago.

'Any man drives off a Sunday and leaves his wife walk to Service is a poor breed of man.'

'He had cause maybe, in his own mind.'

'What cause? What's he ever done for her or you?'

'Pay bills.'

'Ten pound a week this thirty years, what's that now, only for you son the farm would have been sold off long ago; you know that, I know that.'

'He works, George.'

'Not real work, not like you or me.'

'He helps, when he's home.'

'When's that? Tinker, footer, travel, talk? Drink in Papist houses, and doesn't give an ass's fart when his first-born marries one of *them*, went to the weddin' in *their* church, and your mother at home near astray in the head, what sort of man's that?'

Eric moved from the table. 'I'd as lief you didn't talk this way George.'

'Afeered of the truth, son?'

'He's my father.'

'And Sam's?' George paused and added quietly; 'and more.'

Eric said nothing for a moment and then: 'You better say what you mean, George.'

'She's been abused, your mother, that's what I mean.'

Odd times, maybe twice a year, his father went on three-day benders. Twice in the last six months Eric had collected him, once from a pub in Blayney, and last time from a boarding house in Armagh. George drank every day. He despised men who couldn't hold their drink, and keep their feet.

'Don't you want to hear, son?'

Eric stared, he wanted to say yes and no.

'It's time you heard.'

The limestone eyes jerked round from the window: 'That eegit son of Maggie Reilly's, that's your half-brother . . . true.'

It was like a sharp slap on the face from a cold heavy hand.

'You know what you're saying, George.'

'I do. From his own mouth I got it eighteen years back, after the fair at 'Skea. We both had a drop taken, I put it to him square, and he didn't deny it. I tould him then if I ever got hint of the like again I'd kill him stone dead and I meant it. That's why he hates me.'

Maggie had been working at Drumhowl since he was born, and every week since he could remember. Eric tried to shape the question in his mind, George answered it before he could ask.

'Every man and woman for miles around knows, bar you, Sam and your mother, and she must half know, that's what has her the way she is.'

Eric went to the small back window that looked north. He could see Robinson's Vauxhall coming down the steep lane from Drumhowl. Joe and Rachel? The whole country?

'You shouldn't have said that, George.'

'Time you heard, son.'

'Why tell it?'

''Cause you don't back her. Now you know what she suffered, still suffers, that fat sow waddling up every mornin' for her milk, workin' around the house, twice a week, sickens me to my stomach to think of it.'

George got up and poured himself a measure of Bush-mills whiskey.

'Don't take it too hard.'

'I don't believe it, George.'

There was a pause. The side of George's mouth went

47

down a little. For a moment he seemed almost angry, then he turned with a shrug.

'Would I lie about a thing like that? Ask him, your father, tell him what I said, see what he says.'

In the half circle of gravel before Inver Hall he could see about a dozen cars including their old Bedford. A speedboat bounced on the water about a hundred yards from the shore, two skiers making a pattern behind it. After dinner with his mother, he was evasive about checking a heifer. From her eyes he could feel she suspected. Had he said he was going to join the hunt at Inver she would have asked him not to go, and he would have agreed. Because of what George had told him this mild deception cut sharply. Her face was still in his mind. As he walked through the parkland he could see his father clearly now with local huntsmen and farmers on the stretch of lawn between the eighteenth-century house and the lake, wee Willy Reilly amongst them, wearing the silly knitted cap like a tea cosy he wore summer and winter. The stables and yard were separate from the house, the otter pack whimpering, scraping at the wrought-iron gates, like big rough-haired fox-hounds.

Two-stepping down the granite steps in black Aran sweater, grey flannels and shabby tennis shoes, Colonel Armstrong came clapping his hands for attention, directing his voice to the local huntsmen:

'Sherry, tea and seed cake inside before we start, the hunt begins at three sharp.'

The voice across the lawn seemed to cut the out-board to silence, the two skiers skimming ropeless towards the shallow gravel. There was hesitation for a moment, then simultaneous mutters.

'Dammit, that's nice?'

'Aye.'

'Why not, sir?'

'That's a dacent notion.'

Of the dozen local huntsmen three were Catholics including Willie Reilly. The Colonel said: 'Dogs not of the pack should, I think, be kept on leash, or tied until we see how they behave.'

More muttered agreement. Small boys and youths were left in charge of the dogs. The huntsmen moved towards the house, his father talking easily with the Colonel. He had the casual self-respect of a farmer tradesman working over thirty years through the country; tinker or gentry, papist or postman, he was the same with them all, a man seemingly without worries. Robinson's Vauxhall was not among the cars. His father seeing Eric approach put up a long arm and pointed towards the house. Eric signalled back, but decided to wait for Joe. He watched the skiers tinkering at the outboard motor, till he heard the car. He was surprised and pleased to see Rachel beside Joe. She wound down the side window.

'Might as well see an otter killed before one of you get it.'

'Is your father here?' Joe asked.

Eric nodded to the house. 'Inside.'

'Posh,' Rachel said.

'Sherry, tea and seed cake.'

'Parlour or pantry?' Rachel asked.

Eric shrugged and smiled. She seemed petulant, looking at the skiers and the lake.

'Do we have to go in?'

'Unmannerly not to.'

'Would they notice or care?'

'We'll go in,' Joe said, getting out. 'I like to hear them talk.'

He walked towards the steps.

'Can't stand her,' Rachel said.

'Who?'

'The Colonel's wife . . . They'll put us down in some poke with a bottle of cooking sherry.'

'They're all right,' Eric said.

'With two thousand acres they'd need to be.'

He had helped here at threshing as a boy. Armstrongs' arrogance was natural. It was the way they were bred, and the Colonel had obliged him in different ways, loaning him farm machinery and a Friesian bull. The flagged hall went the length of the house, a wide slow-raked staircase, walls hung with military portraits, and strong faced women; couches, odd shaped chairs and garden furniture round the walls, a central refectory table, decanters of sherry, teacups and a canteen type tea pot with two handles. There were about thirty people in all, locals grouped separately in a corner baiting Willie Reilly. Joe had joined them. Eric could hear his father laughing. He paused with Rachel at a games table midway between the local group and some of the house party. The American with the steel-rimmed glasses was talking to the Colonel's daughter, beside them the Pack-master. He looked a bit like Harold Wilson. Then he saw Maggie Reilly coming out behind the staircase with a steaming steel container. As she walked to the table his father leaned towards her and said something. Maggie smiled. Eric felt suddenly embarrassed and uncomfortable. His father's voice was easy and teasing at Willie Reilly:

'Thon wee brown bitch of yours, Willie, what happened her ear?'

'I et it,' Willie said.

There was a burst of laughter. With his slightly mongoloid face, the stutter and blue knit beret, he was a

natural target for yeomanry unease in gentry surround-
ings:

'What odds about her ear, she's got the best nose in
the country.'

Someone said: 'She's very small, Willie, very small.'

'Hardy, well bred, and fast, and she'll stick to the
river, just you watch, not like some big auld mongrels
I'll not mention.'

Another said: 'If an otter got a good grip on her,
Willie, he'd pull her under.'

'Would you think that, Petey?'

'I would, Willie.'

'That big dog of yours John, what do you call him?'

'Blister.'

'Aye . . . Blister . . . pity he's blind.'

The laughter turned from Willie. Eric heard his father
chuckle.

'He can see a mile off, Willie, and he can smell
further.'

'But will he hunt with the pack, John?'

'Ahead of them, Willie.'

There was a slight burr in his father's voice. He had
spent the morning in a pub somewhere. Eric felt a revulsion now he had not thought possible.

The Colonel was going around with a tray of sherries
and a decanter, his wife following with a plate of cut
seed cake. The Colonel asked Rachel:
'Sherry or tea, dear?'

'Sherry, please.'

'Eric?'

'Tea, please.'

The Colonel called over: 'Tea here, Maggie.'

Mrs Armstrong held out a plate of seed cake. She
looked at Eric with unfocused, brown eyes and smiled
as he took a slice of cake, then moved on to Rachel.

Maggie came waddling over and filled Eric's tea cup. There was a slight tremor in his hand.

'You look awful worried, Eric?'

Rachel said: 'He got a love letter this morning Maggie.'

Maggie frowned and said: 'Some playboy sent that, pass no remarks.'

When Maggie moved away Rachel asked: 'Are you all right?'

'Yes.'

'What's wrong? Do you want to go out?'

'No.'

Gradually the quickness of his heart slowed. The people in the hall seemed glazed. He sat on the side of an armchair, his teacup on the games table. Rachel leaned towards him and said quietly:

'I love you.'

He looked at her and said: 'And I you . . . something come over me, I'm sorry.'

'What?'

'Nothing, I'll tell you after.'

The American was saying to the Colonel's wife: 'Yes but the kill is a fact of nature, Harriet, and nature plays sick jokes on all of us, like blindness, right? Old age? War? Death?'

'Brother Rat St. Francis said, likewise Brother Otter.' She smiled oddly.

'Was he sane?'

'The greatest human being since Christ. Have you read Chekhov's *Ward No. 6*?'

'No.'

'About a doctor in an asylum who realises as he goes mad that sanity is locked away and lunatics outside run the world . . . '

'Odd notion!'

'Probably true.'

'You're joking, Harriet!'

'If they were in charge history might make more sense!'

'History would end!'

'A consummation devoutly to be wished.'

The American laughed. The Colonel was among the locals again, refilling proffered glasses. He dropped his voice and said to Eric's father:

'This Packmaster isn't over keen on local hounds joining the pack; if dogs get out of hand some of you may have to put them on leash or withdraw them, you understand.'

'Aye surely, Colonel.'

'That makes sense.'

'We're not here to spoil the sport,' his father said.

Willie Reilly stuttered, 'My wee bitch will hunt with any pack, she'll stick with the best of them Colonel.'

'I hope she does, Willie.'

'She's killed otters, and foxes and hares, and an auld badger dog, big as a boar, that's what happened her ear.'

'There must be a drop of the tiger in her, Willie.'

Laughter caused all heads to turn in the direction of the locals.

'Yes'll not laugh when ye see her workin'.'

The Colonel moved towards the Packmaster and had a word with him. He looked at his wrist watch and said:

'We'll have to make a start.'

Locals and guests followed him towards the big double door. Only the Colonel's wife remained. She stood at the refectory table, with the same odd smile.

The iron gates of the yard were opened. The otter hounds came whimpering and whining on to the sloping lawn, smelling and snarling round local hounds. Blister stood rigid as the pack nosed warily round him. The

Packmaster shouted something, the Whipmaster cracked his whip for order. As Rachel and Eric walked across the gravel to the lawn, Rachel asked:

'Do you want to tell me what got you inside?'

Eric was watching the dogs. 'The auld fellow and Maggie Reilly.'

There was a ten second silence before she said: 'That's a long way back.'

'How long have you known?'

'School, I didn't rightly believe it 'till I heard them at home one night.'

She paused and looked up at him. 'You never guessed?'

'Nothin' till George this morning.'

'So?'

'My mother, she must know, and that one up every day about our place.'

Rachel stepped up on to the grass and moved ahead of him. She turned. 'Could happen to me.'

'Could it?'

'Any woman . . . or you, like your father.'

Eric shook his head. Willie Reilly was laughing and yapping with excitement. He had unleashed his wee brown bitch. She was making circles in a small area wagging her tail between her legs. The Packmaster was saying something to Willie.

'Because she's Catholic?'

'Maybe. I don't want to think about it.'

'Don't, it's history now.'

John Willie came over smiling, his hat cocked well back.

'Are you childer goin' to talk or walk?'

Rachel asked: 'Will we see any otters killed John?'

'You'll not see an otter, let alone a kill.'

The horn sounded and John Willie moved away, the

Whipmaster in the middle of the dogs, the Packmaster walking ahead with a steel-shod stave, the countrymen with ashpoles, in their dark clothes and caps, coats tied with twine across their shoulders, the house party in colourful gear with an assortment of blackthorn and racing sticks. Now and then the Whipmaster called a dog by name . . . Elvis, Togo, Billy . . . all fanning out, the dogs setting a sharp walking pace. Where the lake narrowed to the river the hunt spread to both banks, the Packleader midstream wading haunch-deep, the Whipper on the northern bank, the otter hounds swimming, plunging, lapping water, testing otter holts, running up and down shallow drains. Where the lake ended, the river went in a slow curve for half a mile. All land north of this was Armstrong land, reclaimed and in good heart, a deep, bog loam, rye grass with tufts of coxfoot, laid out in ten-acre divisions, a herd of over eighty cows grazing in one division, a Friesian bull walking alert through them. Wee Willie's brown bitch had left the river following a hare scent. The bull came trotting towards her, head lowered. She came back cowering to Willie's heels.

'That wee bitch of yours, Willie, she'll kill a bull before the day's out.'

General laughter from the locals as Willie said: 'The day's not done yet.'

He kicked his dog sharply in the ribs. She ran off yelping. The hunt paused to watch Willie running up a ditch after her. Someone said:

'Between them they'll kill a hedgehog!'

The flat land sloped upwards, loamy hillock country, rising sharply thereafter to the gaunt highlands left of Carn Rock, thousands of acres planted with larch and Sitka spruce. Eric saw the American looking up and heard him say to the Colonel:

'It's Greek.'

'It can be beautiful.'

'How far does Inver go?'

'To the forest, ten townlands, but there's shooting rights for some hundreds, some I've never stood in.'

Rachel said to Eric: 'Let's cross.'

The river was knee-deep. They crossed to the southern bank. The sun was high and hot. From this first bend the narrow tributary of the Finn changed character, snaking through boggy rush land, long weedy tendrils waving in the brackish water, broken sedge and froth, tins and plastic bags dammed by a rusting barbed-wire fence from bank to bank, the bric-à-brac of a river dump used by the Grues of Annahullion, Catholics. The dogs swam under the wire. The hunters got out of the river to bypass. The banks were now so steep they had to stay in the river bed or walk the high verge watching from a height. Rachel and Eric kept to the bank. A crane hidden in an area of sedge and bulrushes flapped slowly out, rising gradually, as though in slow motion towards a scrub of alder and stunted thorn. Midstream, John Willie waded alongside the Whipmaster. His eyes did not follow the crane. He was watching Blister who seemed to keep separate and now broke away swimming strongly across a deep dark pool, towards a big leaning forked ash tree cloaked with ivy. At the opening of the fork he gave a screeching yowl partly dispersed by water in his mouth. The otter hounds immediately gave tongue. The horn sounded, all dogs swimming towards the fork, scrabbling to get a grip on the bare tentacles of ash root. The Whipmaster hunkered, slipping sideways down the northern slope, thrusting himself towards the tree, a terrier yapping at his heels. When he reached the trunk he grabbed a root with one hand, the terrier by the scruff of the neck and thrust it into the opening with some rough word of encouragement that sounded like 'g'winn, g'inn'. The terrier went into the hole. All stood, the hounds frustrated at the opening were scrambling up again. The Packmaster followed by John Willie waded chest-deep to the opening and listened, examining the earth for tracks.

The Master shouted: 'One here or was!'

All waited, watching. Nothing. The Whipmaster got up on the tree-trunk, held a branch of ash and jumped up and down on the sloping earth as best he could. Still nothing. Blister had left the pack and gone down the river hunting alone. The American's voice came from the far bank.

'Scent is an astonishing sense.'

The terrier appeared at the opening, shaking a glossy river rat. Rachel giggled with relief. The rat went floating slowly down stream, twitching. Most faces registered disappointment.

'Not quite a trophy,' said the American.

'There was an otter here,' the packmaster called up.

'Could be a quarter of a mile away by now,' the Colonel said.

'I hope it's at Lough Erne,' Rachel whispered and asked: 'Why do they hunt them?'

'They eat trout.'

'So do we. Have you seen one ever?'

'Twice.'

'Killed?'

'No.'

'What are they like?'

'Big water squirrels, brown fluffy fellows, whiskery, with bit tails.'

'They sound nice.'

'They are.'

'Timid?'

'They'll fight if they have to, a whole pack, so they say.'

Unseen by Pack or Whipmasters Blister had worked his way out of sight round another bend. John Willie knew this but did not draw attention to it. The hunt proceeded slowly. There were a lot of holts in this deep section, men and hounds working back and across from one holt to another.

Down river Blister gave tongue. There was a look between Pack and Whipmaster. The hounds replied, scrambling out of the river, bypassing a hundred yards' stretch towards Blister's call. All running now, men, women, huntsmen towards the bend. When they got there it was an arched bridge, a car parked on it. A small round man standing on the parapet waving his cap and shouting something. All running now towards the bridge. The man on the bridge was pointing down towards the pond of a disused scutch mill. House party and hunters crossed the bridge and got down into the shallow water underneath. The man was saying:

'A big otter dog, by Christ he must weigh thirty pounds or more, thon big hound dog of John Willie's near caught him.'

At the bridge the water was two feet deep, deepening gradually as the pond widened. It was deeply ringed with bulrushes, sedge and reeds. Anything moving would be spotted. The mill-race was dammed by three old railway sleepers, the end of the pond a limestone wall. The mill itself had been shattered last year by the I.R.A., U.D.A. or British Army; no one quite knew or at the moment cared. Under the bridge ten men had now formed an underwater barricade of legs by standing close together, moving slowly down the pond prodding ahead with their ashpoles and iron-shod staves. About half the otter hounds were in the pond swimming, the other half hunting the fifty yard stretch of bank and sedge on either side. With a sudden heart stop Eric saw a small brown head emerge in the sedge on the left bank. He was about to shout. Instead he nudged Rachel and pointed with a jerk of his head. Her mouth opened in wonder and pity; she whispered:

'Don't, Eric! Don't! Let it live, let it live.'

As they watched the brown head submerged again. No one else had noticed.

From the cottage above the mill a small hunched figure came down towards the pond, through a half acre of flowering potatoes. Rachel asked:

'Who's he?'

'Dinny McMahon.'

'He has a gun.'

'I can see that.'

'What's he doing?'

'Dunno.'

They watched the figure pushing through the thorn ditch, stumping across a waste of egg-bushes, boortrees and brambles to the clearing at the edge of the pond where the dogs worked and the men and women watched. No one looked round until he aimed his gun at the water and splayed a blast of pellets through the swimming dogs. There were shouts from the men, screams from the women, yelps from a dog. All turned to look at the small man. He split his smoking shotgun, dropped the empty cartridge, put his hand in his pocket and inserted another cartridge. In the silence everyone could hear the click of the hammer going back. The Colonel walked out of the river to face the gunman. Only Eric and Rachel could see the two figures outside the cottage.

'Yes!?' His military voice, a rifle report.

'No,' the little man said, his voice a hard Fermanagh rasp.

'What do you mean? No.'

'That's what I mane, NO . . . Sorr. Colonel . . . I mane go back to the bridge and round the other side.'

'Who are you?'

'Here a thousand years, and the same again, Mc-Mahon, Daniel and this mill-pad is mine, it's my land you stand on, and I say "No" to you, and all like you, and to any of my own race down there in that shuegh with you, none while I breathe is goin' to go down this pad, no means no, and that's that.'

'I see.'

'I'm glad you're not blind, Sorr, I can see rightly too and I want to see you walk back that pad while I stand here.'

An otter hound was whimpering on the bank licking at his flank which seemed bloody and shattered.

'Did you have to fire on the dog?'

'Ah Jasus, is it the poor cratur of a dog, slaverin' to rip a wee otter dog half its size?! Shite talk, Sorr, keep it for your guests at mess in the Hall.'

The hounds had stopped hunting aware of human tension. The chain in the river had slackened. The four women present looked frightened. The Colonel unruffled, his voice iron hard asked:
'Is this the townland of Shanroe?'

'You're on it, Sorr, my part of it, all three acres.'

'I have hunting and shooting rights for this townland and all the townlands from Inver to Corrawhinny.'

'Is that a fact?'

'It is.'

'Well I have shooting rights here in my two hands, that's how you got yours, and if you want now I'll show you how it works.'

He raised his gun and aimed it directly at the Colonel's head. John Willie came up from behind the Colonel both arms outstretched, stepping between the Colonel and the gun.

'Ah now, Dinny, for Christ's sake!'

'Go back, John.'

'Dinny, please listen . . . '

'You listen . . . John, go back, I'm tellin' you.'

Eric felt a contraction in his stomach. The little man said:

'I've nothing against you or yours, John, I only want you and this man to get back to the bridge, and go down the far bank. From there on you can hunt to Enniskillen, you can kill all the otters in Ulster for all I care. What I say is plain and I mane it, and you better tell your friend, the Colonel, that.'

John Willie turned and had a quick-whispered word with the Colonel. The Colonel said to McMahon:

'Do you understand what you are doing now?'

'Do I look a fool?'

The Colonel said nothing to this.

'If I were you, Sorr, I wouldn't think about police let alone mention them. It'd take one of her Majesty's buggerin' Regiments to shift me, you can go in God's good time, or now; if you don't I'll blow the head clane off your shoulders.'

Again John Willie said something to the Colonel. For ten seconds that seemed like a minute the Colonel stared coldly back at the two-barrelled gun, and the ugly hunched little man with one eye closed. When he turned to go back the chain in the river broke, going different ways to the southern bank. The Colonel walked slowly towards the bridge, his face impassive as a boot.

The Colonel's daughter looked very white and shaken. She took his hand. He let her hold it for a

61

moment. As he moved towards the American he passed Sam Heuston who had left the river and was walking towards McMahon.

'I wouldn't,' the Colonel warned.

'I will,' Heuston said and then shouted suddenly at McMahon: 'There's one not afeered; I'll walk this river bank and you'll shoot me dead before I quit: bluff!'

For a moment McMahon stared then spat: 'Scald-crows, weasels aye, and river rats, I'll honour *them* with this.' He tapped the barrel of his gun: 'Not *you* . . . let the Colonel try again or the dogs and you'll see how I bluff.'

At the bridge the American said to the Colonel: 'Interesting.'

The Colonel asked John Willie: 'Do you know him, John?'

'Dinny McMahon, I do Sir, he's half-odd.'

'A lunatic,' the Colonel said. 'We've hunted this stretch before.'

'Before 'sixty-nine,' Courtney said.

Tony Courtney was a Catholic who trained gun-dogs for the Colonel. There was a long pause and then the Colonel said:

'Yes.'

All faces fixed in suppressed anger or embarrassment watched the small hunched figure, ignoring Heuston's taunts, walk back through the potato patch towards the cottage. The Colonel asked:

'Whose dog is grained?'

The Whipmaster said: 'One of the pack.'

'Better take it to the vet . . . whose car is this?'

The man who waved on the bridge said: 'I'll take the dog, Sir.'

The dog's leg was badly shattered. The Whipmaster lifted the dog into the back seat of the car and got in beside it. The car drove off. The rest of the pack were walking about the bridge, some still shivering with excitement, others looking intently up at the human faces. From a mass of bulrushes near the mill-race there was a brown splashy leap, a quick scrabble and the otter was over the rotting sleepers and swimming down the mill-race towards the steel structure of the wheel. In a few seconds it would be in open river again and away. If anyone noticed apart from Eric they made no mention. The Colonel said:

'No point in standing about.'

The Packmaster said: 'Can't we walk down the left bank and hunt on?'

The Colonel said bluntly: 'No. We'll go back, trailer the dogs and hunt Mullivam.'

There were general murmurs:

'You're right, Colonel.'

'Wouldn't plaze him.'

Sam Heuston back from his confrontation said: 'If I had my way I'd bury him alive and hunt on.'

'I don't want talk like that . . . ' the Colonel said.

'I don't want talk either,' Heuston said, 'I'd do it.'

'Trivial . . . ' the Colonel said . . . 'we'll forget all this and go.'

'I'll not forget it . . . ' Heuston said.

Courtney and the other Catholic farmers looked very tense.

'I'm sorry,' the Colonel said to Courtney.

With a glance he included the other Catholic huntsmen. Heuston said:

'I'm not sorry.'

The Colonel said: 'I'm not afraid to use a gun, Sam, or face one, but I reject that sort of thinking.'

He jerked his head towards the McMahon cottage: 'You're talking his language.'

Heuston said: 'And look where it's got them, look where it's left us, twenty men on a bridge afeered to cross because of a wee man with a gun, afeered to tell police, for fear we'd be blown up or burnt out . . . you think about that, Colonel, hard, 'cause you'll have to sooner than you think.'

He snapped his fingers, and walked off, followed by a mongrel hound. Joe said quietly to Eric:

'He'd get on well with your Uncle George.'

Eric said: 'They drink together.'

John Willie came over and Rachel said: 'For a moment I thought he was going to shoot.'

John Willie shook his head and smiled.

'He's waited years for that, and he'll put in the rest of his life telling about it.'

Rachel said: 'It didn't look that funny from here.'

'You two coming to Mullivam?'

Before Eric could answer Rachel said: 'No.'

Joe said as he left with John: 'See you to-night, Eric.'

'Right.'

From the bridge they watched the hunt spread back up the river 'till it went out of sight. Rachel took the ash rod Eric had broken off on his way down the river and threw it into the water. They watched it float down and stop against the dam. Rachel said:

'Let's go home by the fields.'

From Shanroe bridge to Tattnagolan was about four miles as the crow flies. They climbed across a wooden bridge into Sam Foster's farm, unreclaimed bottom land, sprit, rushes and rough tussocks growing them a heavy morass, snipe twisting and wheeling away as they walked, white clouds drifting north towards the fields under Carn Rock. They stopped at Foster's well, a clean stone arched well, white-washed with a glitter of gravel in the bottom, so clear they could see spiders and tiny creatures walking on the surface. As they were about to drink they paused and turned to look. From half a mile they could hear the great wing beats. Two swans came down the river from Inver, flying low over the mill, heads craned for Lough Erne. They stared as though they had never seen swans fly before.

'So beautiful,' Rachel said, then added, 'but so ugly . . . the world.'

'You're not.'

'How I feel is . . . the hunt, and that little man, a thing like that, I get sick with hate, fear or both.'

They drank from a tin porringer, chained by its handle to the wall of the well. For minutes they sat in silence looking. Then Rachel said:

'At home I listened . . . I thought they're wrong my parents, because we had Catholic neighbours. I didn't want to hate them, and I didn't, but in the delivery ward in April some time they were mostly Catholics. I heard them talk, so coarse and stupid, holy magazines and rosaries and this fuzzy-headed priest going about blessing their labours and their babies, and the horrid way they sucked up to him.' She paused: 'Even I didn't hear what I heard at home, I couldn't live with them or work with them because . . . ' She paused again and shrugged . . . 'Last night those animals . . . their husbands . . . sons, brothers, cousins; they do hate us, you can feel it.'

For a moment Eric was silent and then: 'I've seen them look at me in streets, marts, I don't want to hate or kill any of them, but a body must do something when the thing's gone the way it has.'

'Get out.'

'I can't.'

'If you don't, you'll . . . '

'We can't run out, we're farmers. I love these fields.'

'More than me?'

'We *made* this country, they *are* this country and know it, they won't rest 'till they bury us or make us part of themselves. Like you I don't want that, maybe that's why I joined, though I'm not sure now.'

'We didn't ask to be born here, I don't want to stay here now.'

'Nor me.'

'Can I tell you something?'

'Anything.'

'It's ugly.'

'If it's about you it's not.'

'It's ugly . . . I was on night duty a month ago, infant wards, all Catholics, in the middle of the night I thought . . . '

'Go on . . . '

'I thought if I set fire to it they'd all be burned, about thirty less of them.'

There was quite a silence before Eric asked: 'Dreamt or thought?'

'Thought Eric, thought. I was tired, I wouldn't do it in a million years, but I did think about it, how I'd start the fire, make it seem accidental, and when I knew what I was thinking, I got so frightened I almost got sick. That's why I'm leaving after midwifery. We're sick Eric, they're sick, and we don't know what to do, I want to believe in God, I can't, I want to be happy, I can't . . . Look around, look, Eric, it's beautiful . . . you are too . . . you are!'

She looked intently at the nail of her left thumb and said: 'You've never touched me ever, why?'

He was so startled when he realised what she meant, that he said without thinking: 'It's wrongful.'

'Yourself, have you touched yourself, ever?'

He heard himself mutter: 'Of course.'

He knew, without looking at her face, that her heart was thumping.

'Me too, more wrongful that, when we love each other.'

He glanced up; her face was tense: 'No, don't look away, Eric. I'm shy too. Along the river I thought, I'll talk today, say what's in my head, ask him, tell him, and . . .'

'I know.'

'You don't because . . .'

'Yes I do . . .'

She stopped suddenly. The questions had come cramped and awkward from her mouth that always had two answers where he could seldom stammer one. Her mind, quick and contrary seemed more frightening to him than her body, untouchable in the old Bedford smelling of pigs, or cinemas reeking of perfumed Jeyes Fluid. He had hardly ever kissed her without embarrassment and awkwardness, believing what his mother told him often.

'You say so little, Eric, I don't rightly know what you think.'

'I don't rightly know myself.'

'Then I'll ask again; you've never touched me, why?'

'It's for begetting. I believe that.'

'And love?'

'In wedlock.'

She shrugged and stood suddenly. 'Let's walk.'

He followed, angry with her, with himself. You could read up about politics, farming and veterinary, learn from experience and mistakes. What book could explain this girl to him or his mother. She was ahead of him, alongside a ditch of foxgloves and double-combed bracken, walking soft as a cat, her jeans clinging from ankle to knee. She turned and said:

'I shouldn't talk that way, it's too forward.'

'Better than treacle talk, but I don't want to feel stupid: I want to understand.'

'Only for you I'd hate men . . . all men, you make me feel special.'

'You are.'

'Far from it.'

'To me, you are.'

She was staring at him. Then she was crying. She took his hands and put them to her face. He could feel her kissing his hands.

'Why are you crying, Rachel?'

'I don't know.'

The brindle heifer was not with the cows nor in the beech copse. He went to the Fortfield, three stripgrazed acres topped by a circle of ash, thorn and hazel. The heifer was on her side pressing in a mass of nettles and docks, the forelegs and nose of the calf protruding. He spoke to her gently strapping his belt round the slimey forelegs. With a foot on her hinchbone he pulled steady for five minutes. The head slipped, coming inch by inch, tongue out. He rested, his body wet from tension. Another five minutes and the shoulders were clear, then the whole calf, slurping out. He slapped it sharply on the ribs, cleared its throat with his forefinger and stood it on splayed shaky legs. Then the heifer was on her feet, spilling afterbirth. He sat on stone, and watched the calf nosing round till it found the warm udder, a teat to suckle. He wiped his hands with dockleaves. Birthsmell, rich warm and milky mixed with rank odour of nettles: and man hath nothing more than beasts. All things go to one place: of earth they are made; to earth they return together. But they knew nothing of love or hate, tithes or time, the packer's knife, the knacker's lorry. And what did he fear? Death? What differ when the body chilled, now of a sudden or slowly in a cockloft fifty years from now? And what did he think she had asked. Not much of this life as he knew it, less of what comes after. Afraid more of living than dying. A coward's mind? Rightly or wrongly it was what he thought. And love? The warm secrets of her body which he feared to touch would cool to clods with bones and rusted mountings; her children, and her children's children walking the same pad.

He left the calf suckling and walked the cows from the river bottoms round the lower end of the house field, approaching the yard from the front of the house. His mother came out in wellingtons to open the gate. She would see his pants were wet from the river and ask. Should he lie or tell? The truth would hurt; the lie more deeply if she heard later.

'Were you in the sheugh, son?'

'I followed dogs with Joe and Rachel.'

'A hunt?'

'Yes.'

She helped him tie the cows.

'Was your father there?'

'Yes.'

'Where is he now?'

'Up Mullivam way; we left after an hour.'

She said nothing and went back to the house. Spooning an egg at table he caught her eye.

'You said you were going to check the heifer.'

'I was, she's calved, a white-head bull.'

'You knew about the hunt, that's the same as a lie.'

'Is it?'

'He's always lying. I don't believe a word comes from his mouth and that hurts; you don't lie to someone you feel for.'

'No but . . . '

'Do you, son?'

'No.'

'I'd as lief you wouldn't hunt God's creatures of a Sunday or any day, but I wouldn't interfere, would I?'

'No,' he lied and finished his egg in silence.

'Why don't you talk, son?'

'Thinking.'

''Bout what?'

'What you said.'

'Lies?'

'Aye, and Sunday . . . God's creatures.'

He couldn't say what he thought. By ten-thirty he had to be in uniform, then drive with George to the U.D.R. Head Quarters at Lisnaskea. They would be stopping and searching cars 'till four in the morning. He drank his tea and looked out at the slow twilight:

'You think I am a hypocrite?'

'What?'

'You heard.'

'Yes I heard, Mother.'

'Because I pray but won't see her, Sam's,' she paused dropping her voice before she said 'wife.'

Eric shrugged. She went on:

'It's wrongful I know, and I've prayed God to help me but . . . the children of my first born . . . Papists . . . and Maggie Reilly pleased to tell me there's another coming . . . God help him . . . I shouldn't say this but I think it . . . I'd sooner he was dead.'

'You don't mean that, Mother?'

'There are things you don't know, son: the joke now is a good person . . . the world's gone bad . . . we should beget as God intended, work hard and pray . . . that's what I was taught: I believe it, I abide by it.'

Eric found the contradiction painful. Very quietly he said: 'And love our neighbour?'

'Those who murder! ... Only Christ himself could do that ... other ways I try to be honest ... kept my marriage vows, reared you boys and run this house for a man who used me unnatural from the start ... and false from the start.'

It was time to go. Eric stood. When he had kissed his mother she said:

'I don't want to be the way I was this morning. Ever ... because I love you, son, and your father, as much as he hates me.'

'He doesn't hate you.'

'Worse ... he doesn't care.'

It was near dark at Oakfield when George came out in uniform. He slumped in the front seat of the Bedford, thrusting a rifle between the seats. Eric put on parking lights and drove the twisting hump-backed lane towards the county road. In the soft, grey dusk there was a herd of cows on the road, Willie Reilly in front with a torch. He pretended not to recognise Eric's van. As the cows passed the man at the back moved towards the car. Cassidy. Eric wound down the window.

'Eric.'

'Martin.'

'How's George?'

'I know how I am and how *you* are!'

McMahon's stand at Shanroe bridge was already local legend. Eric could see Cassidy smiling in the faint light of the dash.

'I hear Willie's wee bitch disgraced him today?'

'Reilly's dog wasn't the only thing happened today,' George said.

There was a moment of silence and then Cassidy said: 'There's a bomb scare in 'Skea.'

'How do you know that?' George asked.

'Radio.'

'We'd better move son.'

As they drove away George said: 'A cog in the murder gang, one of your Yankee mafia, I mind him bare foot, his auld fella out for hire, tricked his way into Protestant land.'

'You don't know that, George.'

'Catholic and Civil Rights, isn't he? . . . Seen him two years ago on the platform in Derry with that wee whore Devlin. See the way he smiled. He's laughin' at us; every bomb that goes off, every man that's maimed or murdered, laughin' 'cause they think we're afeered. No balls, that's what they say to therselves. He knows who sent that note, knows where, when and how you'll be got, it's all linked: Rome, politics, America, gunmen. In Christ's name how did he get money to buy Protestant land and pay two prices for it, a back-hander to a crooked solicitor and some lundy to bid; and them cows! The whole shute must come to near £30,000!'

'Borrowed, he works hard, George.'

'Murder money; they're diggin' graves for us night and day and we're standin' lookin' at them like the Jews in Europe; they've got their score to settle and they mean to settle once and for all; if we let them.'

A scaldcrow feeding on the carcass of a run-over dog flapped away as they passed in the growing dark.

'We bate them before: we'll bate them again.'

Two miles from Lisnaskea they could see flames and ragged smoke over the town.

'Cassidy's bomb,' George said.

A British Army patrol stopped them. They showed their papers, a soldier said:

'One of your mates got it an hour ago.'

'Where?'

The soldier called back to the radio jeep: 'Where were the father and son got?'

A voice called back: 'Tatnagone.'

Eric's heart stopped. There were only three families in the townland of Tatnagone.

'Name?'

'Robinson.'

Eric heard himself ask: 'How?'

'Gunned in a car at the house; the son's dead.'

Eric could feel his body shaking. He drove slowly into Lisnaskea past a burning supermarket, two fire brigades, black helmeted figures, the garish street, Saracens and shattered glass, debris, soldiers, a siren moaning, huddled groups in the doorways; people sweeping up glass, a draper's dummy headless in a shop window. George said:

'Someone must pay.'

There were about a dozen cars at Robinsons', two black R.U.C. patrol cars, a U.D.R. jeep, and overhead a helicopter with a powerful beam scanning fields and ditches. As he got out of the van George said loudly:

'Mick Cunningham's car! What's he here for?'

'He lives two fields away,' Eric said.

'What's he here for?'

'It's no time for shouting, George.'

Dixon the Commandant said: 'George, we don't want guns in a dead house, leave it in the van.'

George made a kind of whining noise: 'For Christ's sake what are guns for?'

Dixon said: 'You take no gun, you can stand out here with your gun if you want!'

George handed his gun to another U.D.R. man. Dixon answered Eric quietly:

'About an hour ago Cunningham heard the shot and got on the 'phone, we were here in ten minutes.'

'Old Tom?'

'In the head, unconscious; poor chance. Joe died outright.'

Eric had seen this kitchen often in a dream, the black police uniforms, British soldiers, Ruth Robinson on a chair by the stove delirious with grief, two other neighbour women trying to comfort her, a superintendent taking notes. In a corner Mick Cunningham, a tall balding Catholic with a heron's neck and the eyes of a rabbit. Eric had bought a suck calf off him two years ago, a big, harmless fellow with a shrill voice. From where he stood Eric could see into the parlour, Joe's boots level with a pot plant in the window, Bryson the undertaker measuring. As he moved towards the parlour door he saw George edge like a coiled spring towards Cunningham. Whatever he said it was as though he had struck him in the mouth. Cunningham jerked a nod and moved sideways towards the front door. Eric paused to let Bryson out.

The body was sheeted, Rachel sitting on a stiff parlour chair at Joe's head, no expression on her face. She turned as he came in. He put a hand on her shoulder. He could feel her trembling. Say something he thought, 'What?' 'Your trouble?' Pray! Kneel! He heard himself say:

'Where?'

'What?'

He nodded at the body.

'Nothing, doesn't matter.'

'Where was he hit?'

She indicated the covered face and said: 'You won't know him.'

He knelt. No prayer came to mind. He knew only

74

that he was alive and that Joe was dead, and was so ashamed of thinking this he said quietly:

'I'm sorry, Rachel.'

Then George was standing opposite. He lifted the sheet and Eric saw Joe's face, a mass of congested blood, unrecognisable. From Joe's dead face he looked up at George and said:

'Cover him, for Christ's sake cover him.'

He felt Rachel leaning against him. George stood and stared. Eric was trying to hold and lift Rachel and pull the cover.

'For pity's sake, George.'

'For pity's sake, I want to see this proper, and I want to mind it.'

Rachel had fainted. There was a door off the parlour, a bedroom probably. He got it opened and managed to get the switch. Striped pink and white paper, a deal floor, brass bed, a corner wash stand. He placed her on the bed.

Her face was so cold that he put his hand to her mouth; breathing all right. Her hands seemed grey. He took them in his own. When her eyes opened she stared at the electric bulb, frightened animal eyes that slowly swivelled and then there was such pain and anguish and ravaged incomprehension that it cut more deeply than Joe's awful face in the next room. If there was a living man could speak now, what words would he use. Christ in Heaven, what were they, who could speak? Say what? Joe, her father, the awful choking sound of the mother two rooms away, George staring stupidly, what words? And because her face was still and her eyes pouring over, it was worse because she made no sound. If she cried out he could say 'Don't Rachel' or 'Please' or some word of solace, but there was no word or words, and he knew it and she knew it, and he knew he was

75

crying with her for Joe, for her mother and father, for
the whole world. Her lips seemed to move and then she
said:

'Loved him, Eric.'

'I know.'

'Loved . . . he was like . . . '

'Yes.'

'Comfort, we're dying . . . love me.'

'I know.'

'Dying, Eric.'

'I know.'

And the cry that came from her mouth, he had never
heard before, and never wanted to hear again. She made
a sort of noise, like something choking. It seemed to
come more from her lungs than throat as though she
were drowning in grief. He held her.

'I'm breaking inside, Eric, breaking, kiss me, touch
me, touch me, love me, comfort me.'

As he held her she went limp. He laid her gently
down. Her face seemed whiter than the pillow. She
looked dead. Then he heard George shouting. In the
silence that followed he went through the parlour. More
people in the kitchen now, the R.U.C. District Inspector
talking with the Sergeant, Ruth Robinson still stupefied
in a chair, the other two women passing round cups of
tea. George was staring hard at the superintendent. Then
he said with a voice as cold as a chisel:

'One of your rotten breed done this.'

The Inspector, a Catholic, did not react.

'Are you deaf?' George shouted, 'Yes, you!'

When George said again: 'Are you deaf?' the tension
altered from grief to a confused hatred. The Inspector
turned and said coldly:

'Who's your Commanding Officer?'

No one answered. Then Eric said quietly: 'Come on, George.'

'Who is your boss?' George asked. 'One of them Kennedys and their rotten mafia?'

The Inspector turned and said to his Sergeant: 'Get this man's Commanding Officer.'

It seemed to Eric that the two women, the Sergeant and the policeman, were all looking at the Inspector with hatred and suspicion. When the Sergeant moved to get Dixon, George said:

'All the one, all murderers.'

The Inspector put down his notebook on the sideboard and waited. When Bill Dixon, George's Commandant came in, the Inspector asked quietly:

'Is this man under you?'

'He is, Sir.'

'Name?'

'George Hawthorne.'

'He has called me a murderer. I have taken note of that, I want you to take note of it and report it.'

'I'm not afeered to say what's true.'

'Outside, George,' Dixon said, ' . . . outside.'

George left, Eric followed. In the yard Dixon took hold of George's arm and said:

'Talk like that does no good, George.'

'You're right, talk's useless, Craig's right. Liquidate them, every last one of them.'

'Listen, George.'

'Too long we've listened, three years too long.'

George wrenched himself away and moved towards the van. Dixon said quietly to Eric:

'Things are bad enough here, take him home, stay with him 'till he cools, that's duty enough for tonight.'

Near their van a British soldier was listening to a small pocket transistor. The voice came across the sea, cold and factual: 'Word has just come in now that Tom Robinson, father of Joe Robinson the part time U.D.R. man who was shot earlier this evening, has also died.'

The voice went on about oil shortages and President Nixon. In the turf shed Eric saw the machine-gunned Vauxhall, Army ballistic experts examining it with a powerful torch. He could see blood splattered on the windscreen. More cars had arrived, military, police and private cars, neighbours standing about in groups, not wanting to go in, knowing they must. He saw a British Army officer walking towards the door with a priest. When the priest went into Robinsons, one of the women began to scream something; it sounded like 'Fenian Bastards, Murderers!' he was glad George was in the van and not in the house. He started the engine and drove slowly through the lighted yard and the uniformed figures, towards the main road.

'Left, take the low road,' George said.

For a moment Eric hesitated; it was two miles longer, but he was not going to argue. He turned left. For miles not a word was said. They were stopped twice at Army checkpoints and quickly cleared. At Latgallon quarries, George said:

'Pull in here.'

'What?'

'I have to stoop.'

Eric drew in behind a gravel dumper. Mid way in the cratered quarry of crags, rock face, and jutting limestone rose the black scaffold of a grading machine, topped by a hut. Beyond it and below five acres of worked over quarry and rock pools, the fields sloped upwards towards Latgallon. George got out and went over behind the dumper. Eric checked that both rifles were still in the car. A dog barked somewhere, a military convoy passed. George was taking his time. When the windscreen got muggy, Eric got out and saw the figure of a man against the sky at the far end of the quarry. The figure was clear of the quarry, and moving in an upland field towards Latgallon. 'Oh God no,' Eric thought, and then called 'George, George!' He cupped his hands and shouted louder 'George!' The figure went out of sight. Eric began to run, tripping over the ragged surface. He fell cutting both hands and a knee. He got up aware of blood dripping from his left hand. He put his left hand in his pocket and kept running. There was a rough staircase of stone hacked out of the quarry face. He went up them two and three at a time. From the quarry top the fields switchbacked up towards Cassidy's. No sign of George, should he call again? Some neighbour, drunk, or courting couple might hear. He was running as in a dream. Two fields from where he was he could see high hedges. He crossed a gate into the lane. He could then see the lights in Cassidy's yard, the reconstructed cottage, the new barns, byres and silo pit.

As he approached the familiar hum of an Alfa-Laval milking pump, the smell of fermenting silage. No sign of George. He kept running 'till he came to a padlocked gate. He clambered across it. The lane forked two ways, one to the house in darkness, the other to the lighted yard. He could see cows tied in cudding in the herring-bone parlour. At the yard entry between two out-houses, he saw what looked like two sacks of meal lying sideways on top of each other. As he neared, with a sudden sick shock, he saw Willie Reilly humped across a bag of dairy nuts, sprawled as though copulating in an obscene posture of death, mouth and eyes open, tongue out. In the yard, he saw George from the back, driving a graip into what looked like a dungheap; again and again and again, and again.

'George!'

Under the 200 watt bulb his uncle's face looked back in knotted fury, his mouth drooping. He flung the graip towards the middle of the yard. It spun bouncing and ringing off the concrete, blood on the prongs. Eric saw that it was a man's body face down in the dungheap. George walked to meet him. Eric tried to say something, his voice made no sound.

'Your bastard brother's in the entry, and that's Cassidy . . . two for two and no shot fired, let them equal that and don't stand there like a gom, the job's done.'

Then George was walking out of the yard and down the dark laneway towards the padlocked gate. The body on the dungheap twitched. Eric's heart was pumping so fast he found it difficult to breath. He moved towards the body. Cassidy's profile all right, bloody lacerations on his neck and back. He turned away retching.

In the kitchen at Oakfield George filled two mugs with Bushmills whiskey. He drank his own, filled it again, and pointed at Eric's.

'Drink up, son.'

'I don't drink.'

'Time you started.'

The yellow liquid in the cracked mug was the colour of the manure effluent on Cassidy's face. Eric put his hands on the table to stop them trembling. His left hand was badly cut and swollen. He was aware that George had hung his coat behind the door and was examining it, groping in pockets. He then looked down at his boots, examined the soles, first one, then the other. Black, dry and shining, a little mud on the toe-caps. The limestone eyes stared straight. He came to the table to fill his mug again.

'What are you afeered of?'

He picked up the bottle of whiskey and held it. 'No shake in that hand; my heart's steady as a rock, and my head; I'd do the same tomorrow or next week. They'll all make noises, but our side'll be glad some men had guts to act; blood for blood, this is a celebration son. They won't know it was me, but vengeance is done, the job's a good one.'

Eric stared. He was insane. The country was full of savage talkers on both sides. He had always thought talk was only talk, and that the men of blood were cold, stupid, and silent, hired by men too clever to take risks.

'Say what's in your head.'

'They didn't do it, George.'

'Cassidy knows who done it, not just by name, he knows them, he could hand you a list from here to Portadown of all their murdering heroes, age, rank, how many jobs they done, *he knows*: that's enough for me.'

'Willie; you knew he'd be there?'

'Luck of the draw.'

'Could have been anyone?'

'I'm not in the dock, son.'

'You are!'

George smashed his mug on the black stove and began quietly, his back to Eric:

'I do solemnly swear support for King William the Third Prince of Orange and all heirs of the Crown so long as they support the Protestant religion and Ascendancy and I do further swear, I was not, I am not, nor ever will be a United Irishman nor took oath of secrecy to that Society and on no account will I admit a Roman Catholic and I am now become an Orangeman without fear of bribery or corruption and I will keep a brother's secrets as my own.'

He had turned from the stove. Eric said without looking up: 'Unless in cases of treason or murder.'

'You goin' to whine, go to that papish Inspector, fall on your knees, tell him it was your Uncle George! That what you're going to do?'

'I'll not do that, George.'

'Then for Christ's sake stop niggling, the job's done; we done it well.'

Eric heard the incredulous pitch of his own voice: 'Ah Christ, George, quit!'

'What?'

'We! We! I'm not stupid; you tricked me.'

'I what?'

'Tricked, tricked.'

'Say your say, go on, say it.'

'Dirty . . . yes, dirty, you're bad as the worst of them, you done a rotten thing, and you clean your hands on me.'

'Did I ask you to folly me, one single word, to witness what was done? You follied, you saw, you're not fit to stomach what you saw let alone do it, so now you whine "tricked" . . . you don't know your own mind . . . I do.'

He was at the bottle again. Eric noticed a slight tremor in the pouring hand.

'They're lucky.'

'Who?'

'Joe, Tom, Cassidy and Willie, the dead ones. I'm going.'

Eric began moving towards the door.

'Wait son, stay awhile.'

'For what?'

'Stay, please.'

That long white face pleading. He had never heard that mouth say 'please'. Nausea gave way to a moment of pity:

'For what, George?'

'Don't cry, Eric, Jesus son, don't cry.'

George put a hand on his shoulder and made him sit on a chair.

'Look at me, son, you know me, don't shake your head like that, speak boy, open your mouth, you sat on my knee in this kitchen and . . .'

'George, that's nothing got to do with what we know.'

'We marched together, made hay, cut turf together we . . . I'm George, your mother's brother, your uncle, your friend, you know me, Eric.'

'I thought I did.'

'My life, have you thought on that, no woman, no brother, no close friend ever, wrought on my lone all my days, for what? I have nothin' but this house and forge, a few acres and a stretch of bog but *that* is somethin', land that is somethin' and I've somethin' to tell you.'

'I know too much, George, I don't want to hear any more.'

'Listen son, old Tom's dead, Joe's dead, Rachel and Ruth, think of them, their men gone.'

'I don't want to hear, George.'

'There had to be a reckoning.'

George held the glass of whiskey towards Eric and said: 'Drink, son, you're like a ghost.'

'I don't want to drink or talk of Robinsons, or Cassidys or Catholics or Protestants, or what's goin' to happen or what's not goin' to happen.'

There was a long silence and then George said: 'I'll tell you what's in my head, been meanin' to tell you this long while, no odds about me, I'm for the suit of boards and the clay. I've no money much, but there is this place, and the bog at Kilcrin; it's all yours.'

Eric looked out the window at the dark fields.

'Land's gone mad everywhere, even round here they'll pay three prices for it . . . all yours, from this night on.'

Land, earth, spades, gravediggers, varnished boxes, women stumbling with grief, men crying. The day after tomorrow four burials between the two churches that faced each other across the river. Machines still on the cows at Cassidy's, kicked off by now. Tomorrow some neighbour or the postman would find them in the yard.

'All yours, eight generations of Hawthornes, yours, I mane it.'

Eric did not look at the white blurred face as he said: 'I don't want it.'

'Take care what you say, son.'

'I said it with care, George, I don't want it. Put it on the collection plate, I don't want it.'

'You don't talk to me like that.'

'How should I talk, what's in our heads now? When we wake; when we meet tomorrow; next day; next week? We won't want to meet. I won't want to work this land, any land about here, ever.'

'You're a coward, boy.'

'Yes.'

'You are . . . '

'Yes, all my life, afraid of you, George, afraid to pick between my mother and father, afraid of God, afraid of Catholics, afraid of dark and dreams, afraid to hate or love . . . I'm tired of being afraid . . . but if you're brave George, then I'm a coward like my father and I'll stay one.'

George stood suddenly. 'Your father's son. O'Neill treacherous bloody Irish at the back of it, begrudgers, traitors, turn your back when I need you most.'

George was whining now, mumbling drunk. Eric said:

'I dunno why I'm in this uniform, who I'm fighting, or what the fight's about, and when it blows by I'll be elsewhere, anywhere, I'll do anything, but I'll not go through another night like this, I'd as lief be dead.'

George suddenly shouted: 'You're nothin' to me . . . nothin', on you go, empty dustbins in Hammersmith, join your brother Sam and his whorey Papish wife, that's your future if you lave here.'

Eric felt anger rising: 'And yours, George?'

He left him standing in the kitchen and went out to the van. Then he was aware of George stumbling across the yard towards the driver's window. Eric wound it down.

'Hand back your gun, son, and get to hell out of this country, you're nothin' to me now, do you hear me, nothin'.'

'We're both dead, George, when you're sober you'll see that.'

As he drove down the lane, he could see George in the rear mirror standing swaying against the squat black outline of the forge.

His mother had been crying, his father's face like ash. Both seemed very shaken. His mother said:

'Could have been you, son, and your father, whoever done it, I hope . . . ' Her voice choked off in a sort of noise. 'God help Ruth and Rachel; what are we goin' to do John?'

'Go to Robinsons',' his father said.

His mother said: 'Tell me, son.'

'Nothin' to tell, Joe's dead and old Tom, it's an awful house, they don't know what they're doing, you'd best go and help whatever way you can.'

'Your hands are cut, son, and your knee.'

'I fell.'

'You've been crying, the boy's terrified, John.'

'Not now.'

His father said: 'We'd best go.'

'God help us all.'

'George?'

'Home.'

'You saw him home?'

'That's where I left him.'

Eric knew they were looking at him closely. His mother said: 'The boy's shocked.'

As he looked in his mother's eyes Eric thought: what if I said, I saw your brother up at Cassidy's, he's murdered Martin Cassidy and Willie Reilly, and if you go out to the haggard and look down you'll see the lights are still on about Latgallon, and they'll be on all night. I never want to see your brother George again, or hear stupid quarrels in this house, or hear the news on telly, or see daylight, and if you go up to oakfield now you'll find George three quarters drunk and half mad, and maybe he'll tell you the story himself. His mother came very close to him.

'Are you all right, son?'

'I'm all right mother, I'll wash my hand and put a cloth on it.'

His father said: 'We'll go.'

His mother went up to put on her coat. His father stood and stared at the floor.

'The best people you could meet in a year's travel Joe and Tom Robinson, I've thought some bitter thoughts this last hour. A time like this you start to think, maybe George and your mother are . . . '

He paused, as Eric said sharply: 'They're not right!'

'I wasn't goin' to say that, son, but it's a low thing a killing like that, unmanly, father and son trapped in a car, like rats burned in a cage. I've thought and thought of every Catholic man I know, I can't see one, not one, would do such a thing, then bit by bit I start to doubt, maybe Dinny McMahon, maybe if he had drink taken, then you begin to doubt them all, hate them all, that's what's happening, men who don't want to hate are pushed to it, that's what I was goin' to say.'

When they were gone Eric washed his hand at the kitchen sink, went to his bedroom, took off his uniform, and lay on the bed in his underclothes. An army helicopter moved up from Robinsons', its searchlight scanning the fields between Robinsons' and Cassidy's, probing ditches, hollows, scrub and gap. Could be they'd find Cassidy and Willie before morning. He switched on the transistor waiting for the next bulletin. When it came in ten minutes there was no mention. His mother and father would be back in an hour or less. He couldn't face any more talk about Robinsons'. He tried to lie still and close his eyes. They were pulsing under the lids. His body was trembling. With an effort of will he could stop it, but moments later it would start again. From where he lay he could see the winch gibbet on the gable wall of the byre where he had talked today with Maggie . . . a hundred years ago. When he closed his eyes he could see Willie Reilly across the bag, his tongue out, George like a clip from an old film, ramming away with a steel fork, the crowded kitchen, Rachel's eyes pouring over. All this was more frightening when he closed his eyes. He kept them open and looked out the window again. Then the board ceiling lit up and he heard the engine of the old Bedford, the squeal of the back springs as it crossed the gulley. Silence. Two doors closing, his mother and father talking in the kitchen, then his mother.

'Eric.'

He replied, his voice strange. They were at his door. As the door opened he said: 'Don't put on the light.'

His father came into the room, his mother stood at the doorway. Even from the low light in the hallway he could see how drawn she was. His father said:

'You go on, Sarah.'

To Eric she said: 'Good night, son.'

His father moved to the window: 'The world's a midden, a bloody midden . . . birds are lucky and trees.'

'You were a brave while.'

'We came back by George's.'

He knows, Eric thought, and asked quietly: 'How was he?'

'On the floor in his own vomit. I put him to bed, your mother cleaned up.'

'Did he say much?'

'Raved, something about "Christ in the fields".'

'What?'

'Christ in the fields . . . raving.'

His father moved from the window, sat on the side of Eric's bed and lit a cigarette. 'Sam's well away from it all.'

'Yes.'

'Dead, you're good for nothin' but the ground; I think you should go, son.'

'I will.'

'When?'

'Tomorrow.'

'Where?'

'Across the water, anywhere.'

'You might have to stay a brave while.'

'No odds, I saw and heard enough today, to keep me away a brave while.'

'You're right, try and sleep.'

'And you, Da!'

Two hours 'till daylight. He closed his eyes and turned from the window. A helicopter like a gigantic hawk whirled silently over the beech copse, a searchlight moving from tree to tree. Birds in outline perched in stuffed stillness on black branches. The pelts of badger, fox and otter, battened to trunks. Soldiers and masked men moved in shadows outside the copse. The searchlight moved to the centre of the clearing. From a gibbet over a huge stone hung a cage full of men and women, fear and hatred in their faces. Beside the stone the Rev. John Plumm read soundlessly, solemnly from the Bible. Below him Maggie Reilly, sow-like, confessed to the anus of a curate listening to her leering between his legs, his father behind Maggie on all fours about to mount. The helicopter ascended slowly, the beam of the searchlight widening. Then Cassidy came into the clearing with a Civil Rights banner carrying a statue of Christ with a bleeding heart, Willie Reilly walking behind him in his blue knitted cap. George, crouching behind the stone altar with a long narrow root scobed out as a collection box flailed at Cassidy, smashing his skull, driving the other end of the shaft through Willie's heart. A young British soldier walked into the clearing with a girl. The girl had rosary beads around her neck. They lay down. The soldier began kissing between her legs. She took a Webley from her handbag and shot him three times in the head. Paratroopers directed by a tall British officer ran from skeletal bushes into the clearing. One of them opened the cage hanging from the gibbet. As the men and women came out they were machine-gunned, bodies falling screaming, coughing, spluttering blood. Rachel in nurse's uniform watched, a hand on her groin, her face blank and crying. Sam and Maisie followed by small children approached his mother. His mother's face was white with hatred. She ripped open Maisie's stomach with a bread knife, pulled out a bloody child and smashed its head against the lectern, screaming 'Papist murderers . . . bastards'. Then a great noise of birds, animals and humans, a noise like a gathering storm, and Eric shouting.

And he was sitting up unable to shout, a retching in his throat, the sky livid behind the black winch gibbet on the byre gable. For a minute he sat, his heart jumping in his chest like a caged animal. The house still. Had he shouted or dreamt he shouted? He looked at his pocket-watch, 6.28, two minutes till the news. He closed his mind against what he knew. A summer dawn like any other, sitting on the side of the bed trying not to think of Tatnagone, Oakfield, and Latgallon, looking out beyond the byre to the haggard field, cows cudding ignorant under hedges, swallows skimming low over the humps and hollows of the house field, rain today with that red sky, hay-rot for small upland farmers, growth for lowland silage makers. It must break soon. Police, questioning, back-tracking, threads of uniform on barbed wire and thorn bush, fingerprints on graip and gates, tractor loads of evidence . . .

'George,' he said to himself quietly. 'Oh Jesus, George . . .'

Lying in a stupor in the cockloft or maybe having his first whiskey to greet the coming day. The voice came low on the transistor: 'Miners, Robinsons, a soldier shot dead in Belfast, two bombs in Lurgan, Nixon, nothing.' He dressed quickly and went out to the hallway in his bare feet, avoiding boards that creaked, his father deep asleep, a grey faced, open mouthed corpse. His mother's door closed. Would she wake and call? Silence but for the wall clock in the lower hall beside his grandparents. He stood in the glass porch listening, the tiles cold under his feet, looking at the sloping yard, the out-buildings stepping down. Always this way. It would stay this way for a hundred years or more when he was gone and all forgotten. He felt pity for the two people asleep upstairs in their separate rooms, Rachel sitting at Joe's side with her mother, and along with pity, shame. No fear; there was nothing left to fear.

The van was facing the entry. He let off the hand-brake. It rolled across the dry yard, bounced over the gulley with a squeal and down by the orchard. Well past the beech copse he let it slip into gear. The engine jolted to life. There would be military checkpoints every few miles, soldiers watchful and jumpy. This was it, a dull red glow in the east, the small odd-shaped fields, bushes, rushes, his heart pumping steadily. Desertion? The coward's way? Maybe, who'd know: George?

Christ! He came on them so suddenly he almost braked, two Saracens across the road, about a dozen soldiers, one of them waving him down from a hundred yards or more. His right foot hovered over the brake, the soldiers grouped round the big rubber wheels, all moving now. He could see their faces, the waving soldier moving backwards.

Now! He put his foot on the accelerator, saw them move apart, some go behind the Saracen, others falling on their stomachs. A flash came from the left ditch, glass shattering; pain, and the old Bedford skidding sideways before it lurched tumbling across the ditch, his lungs bursting, dying, yes, dying, blood in mouth and eyes, done, yes, over, and then as the Fermanagh uplands dimmed he heard Yorkshire voices far away, one saying:

'Christ knows, he's Irish, mate; they're all fucking mad over here; shoot first, ask after.'

Victims

Leonard was leaning on the rail of the jumping enclosure watching the entrance. Music had been coming from the speakers since he arrived – 'Land of Hope and Glory' – now competing with the staccato of cantering, jumping horses, the bawling of show cattle, megaphoned instructions from stewards, the squealing of pigs, sudden bursts of applause, the continuous hubbub of talk within and without the licensed marquee.

On a pole above the marquee a Union Jack flapped in the south wind. From it triangular bunting in red, white and blue stretched round the enclosure taking in the judges' platform and a small committee tent. Across the entrance from the road an embroidered cloth read:

WELCOME TO INVER SHOW
GOD SAVE OUR QUEEN

Dark-suited countrymen in hats, caps and boots, their wives in capacious summer wear and strong shoes examined pens of sheep, pigs and fowl, inspected and criticized glossy, prize-winning show cattle, walked through covered stalls of garden and domestic produce, argued cheerfully with salesmen about the merits and defects of gleaming new tractor models and agricultural machinery, or sat about in family groups eating sandwiches, whip-ices or drinking beer in the August sun.

Here and there, jodhpurs, tweed and blatant voice, or casual urban wear allied with a Yorkshire accent marked the presence of gentry, their guests, and British soldiers on unobtrusive day-leave from barracks at Lisnaskea or Roslea.

Nothing much had happened. A horse had broken its leg. Leonard had heard the vet say quietly to the owner:

'It'll have to be destroyed.'

As the last horse cleared the jumps he kept watching the entrance with his good eye. Beyond the showground the sloping meadows of after-grass gave way to the grey-brown brooding of Fermanagh uplands. In the long view detail seemed blurred. In the enclosure a fresh crop of dandelions crocheted in the green sward pulsed with a violence that forced him to look away. He covered his eye with a scarred hand, took out a scrap of paper, read the coded message without expression, put a match to it and dropped the blackened ash.

When he looked up she was in the entrance, waiting, a smallish madonna, composed, with cool all-seeing eyes, her face set in a medieval mould. He waited till she moved, then left the railing and went towards her. Unsmiling, Lynam watched him approach. He had grown a beard which hid the aggressive jut of his lower lip. They did not shake hands as she said:

'It's you.'

'Yes.'

'That much I was told.'

A city girl dressed for summer streets, leather shoulder-bag and sandals. From a battery-powered megaphone a steward announced twice: 'All winning competitors in the beef section to the judges' stand.'

Leonard guided her through the crowd past farmers urging a nervous Friesian bull up the ramp of a trailer, down a grass alley-way of farm produce and display stands towards an open space at the rail of the jumping enclosure directly opposite the judges' platform. He reached in the pocket of his denim jacket for cigarettes. When they were both lit his silence forced her to speak.

'For a friend you are not saying much.'

'Nor you.'

'I know nothing except . . . '

She paused for the megaphoned voice to announce: 'Armstrong Memorial Award for the best beef bull: Samuel Foster of Mullinahone.'

When the ragged applause faded she said: 'A car called at four, an Army Council note, I was to go where I was taken, didn't say where . . . under your command . . . Burke's hand . . . and the driver said nothing between here and Dublin. That's all I know.'

After another announcement she said: 'I was very frightened . . . still am.'

'Of what?'

'A final journey.'

'Nothing like that.'

'You've been briefed, warned, something.'

'I don't believe all I hear.'

'You take orders.'

'Don't you?'

She paused before asking: 'What orders?'

Another announcement greeted with back-slapping and laughter, a popular winner.

'Big house,' Leonard said. 'We hold some gentlefolk till they bring us Quinn, McIntyre, and Fanin from Long Kesh.'

'What big house?'

'Inver Hall, two miles from here . . . that's him,'

Leonard said, with a jerk of his head towards the judges' platform. 'I don't want to point, the tall one, jodhpurs and cloth cap.'

'Who's he?'

'No one ... the young one's his son-in-law. Secretary, Foreign Office.'

As Lynam shrugged Leonard added: 'Also he's an English lord.'

Lynam stared across the enclosure: 'When?'

'Tonight.'

There were three more announcements before she spoke: 'They won't release them.'

'They'll think about it.'

'And if not?'

'We keep our word.'

'How?'

'Does it matter?'

'Will that involve me?'

'You'll be there.'

The spikey growth of bladed grass at her feet seemed terrifying in the golden light. She could feel sweat going down her back.

'And if they bring them?'

'We leave.'

'With the gentry?'

'Till we're clear.'

'Where to?'

'That's fixed.'

'And if they refuse?'

'I've said it.'

For a moment she hesitated before saying: 'Kill them?'

'Execute.'

'Then what?'

'We fight.'

'It's suicidal.'

'Simple and works elsewhere.'

She paused to ensure that her voice would not betray what she felt.

'I didn't volunteer for active service, why me?'

Leonard shrugged.

'Policy?'

'He,   they . . . someone   wants   rid   of me . . . you . . . have you thought of that?'

'Like?'

'Burke.'

Leonard thought about this then shook his head.

Lynam asked: 'And if I refuse now?'

Leonard dropped his cigarette on the grass and covered it with his foot, and asked with more concern than threat: 'Can you?'

When Lynam did not reply Leonard asked: 'Drink?'

'No.'

'Sandwich?'

She shook her head.

'Tea?'

'No . . . thanks.'

'Ice?'

To stop the persistent questions, sort out the awfulness of what he had just told her and steady the unnatural racing of her heart she nodded assent.

She followed him as he made his way towards the whipped ice machine. A woman in charge was adjusting something at the back.

'Two please,' Leonard said.

'In a minute,' the woman said.

Leonard nodded and moved away a few yards. As they waited Lynam looked at him properly for the first time.

'What happened to your eye?'

'Accident.'

'On a job?'

'Yes.'

'Can you see with it?'

'No.'

'I'm sorry.'

He nodded and said: 'And me . . . for your trouble.'

Her face gave nothing away. 'Not much you don't hear.'

When he made a gesture she said: 'Abortion is the word.'

Her mind, he thought again, a clenched fist against pity, maidenhood, motherhood or anything denoting feminine softness. She had climbed fast and high, in a movement dominated by power-hungry men, unafraid of violence and now unsure of her motives. Some felt she secretly despised them and the cause. Drunk once in a Rathmines flat Burke had told him:

'She knows too many dodgy Press boys and politicians . . . calculating as a cat . . . makes love with her eyes open . . . Christ knows what she thinks or believes . . . not in me . . . not in God . . . I've even wondered if she's Special Branch, but I think not.'

At the time Leonard was amused at Burke aligning himself with God, but felt the assessment of Lynam was fairly accurate. He was tempted now to say something unkind. He said:

'It's a bleak word.'

She looked at him steadily for a moment. Like other Northerners she'd met, close; spare with words.

'Almost,' Burke had said, 'as clever as me.'

The reply in her mind did not reach her mouth. She looked over at the woman filling cones and said:

'Your whips are ready.'

A blond man, almost albino, with a tall limber Negro,

both in vivid shirts and jeans, approached the ice-cream stand unaware of Leonard. The Negro spoke:

'Can you give us two love?'

The woman said, nodding towards Lynam and Leonard, 'These were here first.'

The Negro turned: 'Sorry mate.'

'That's OK,' Leonard said.

As they walked away Lynam asked the question with her eyes. Leonard nodded.

'What does he think of it over here?'

'Who?'

'The Negro.'

'He doesn't, he reads the gutter press.'

A tinker woman carrying an infant wrapped in a rug blocked their path. She had reddish hair, bad teeth, glazed eyes, and looked years beyond child-bearing.

'God bless you Sir, Miss, can you spare a copper for a poor baba?'

The child, Lynam thought, looked pallid and sick. As Leonard groped for a coin she asked: 'What age is your baby?'

'Near three month Miss.'

The Colonel approached from the right, and said to her: 'You're welcome my dear but I've already told you twice . . . you must not beg from people.'

'Yes, your Honour.'

As she moved away the Colonel said to Leonard: 'Not charity to give when she spends it all in there.'

He nodded towards the licensed marquee. The Colonel looked directly into Leonard's face then into Lynam's eyes. As he moved off he said: 'Lovely day.'

'It is,' Leonard said.

As they watched him walk away Lynam asked: 'Do you want to kill him?'

'You know the answer, why ask?'

They walked in silence to the enclosure where Lynam asked: 'Deadline?'

'Tomorrow midday.'

'If they refuse . . . what?'

She stopped, unable to frame the question. Leonard answered: 'One on the hour . . . then one every six hours.'

Lynam looked at the whipped ice. A squirt of liquid raspberry on top had run down the cone onto her fingers. She had not tasted it and looked at it now with revulsion.

'How many?'

'Six or eight most nights to dinner.'

'I don't want this.'

Leonard took her whipped ice . . . Everywhere farmers were loading livestock onto trailers and lorries. The Show was over but the presentation of rosettes continued at the judges' platform, punctuated by announcements and scattered clapping. From the speaker the melody of 'The Eton Boating Song' was drowned by the sudden slash of horse-piss on grass as a brown gelding straddled comfortably about ten yards from where they stood. Lynam asked:

'Must we endure this?'

'We can go any time.'

Making their way towards the entrance they passed stalls of garden and domestic produce flanking the marquee. A tall woman with a well structured face and beautiful limbs surrounded by farmers' wives was saying with careful articulation:

'My mother used to add lemon verbena to crab-apple jelly; gives it a wonderfully subtle flavour.'

Leonard said quietly, 'His wife.'

'Whose?'

'Colonel's.'

'She'll be there tonight.'

Leonard nodded and Lynam said: 'She reminds me of someone.'

They walked out of the show-ground, got into a black beetle Volkswagen and drove south towards the border.

The Colonel had shaken many hands, dispensed rosettes, certificates, trophies, Perpetual Cups and Medals of Merit. As he moved towards Alex Boyd-Crawford, George Hawthorne, blacksmith and small farmer approached:

'George?'

'A word Sir.'

George was serious. He had been questioned, the Colonel knew, by the R.U.C. in connection with a double murder three miles from Inver. His nephew Eric O'Neill, a boy of twenty-three and part time soldier in the U.D.R., had been accidentally shot at an Army checkpoint; suicide it was rumoured.

Glazed by grief and whiskey the eyes that stared from that anvil-grey face looked someway blind. The Colonel was prepared to listen briefly:

'Something over here I want you to see,' George was saying and began to walk.

'Yes?'

He was pointing a callused finger at the dry closet left of the entrance with 'Gentlemen' printed over the door.

The Colonel stopped:

'Can't you tell me George . . . some obscenity?'

'I'll say it straight Sir . . . one of our "patrons" shit on the floor and writ above it, "That's what we think of the Brits and their Army . . . up the I.R.A."'

The Colonel's expression did not change.

'Words.'

'Animals . . . turn your stomach.'

'Words, George.'

The Colonel looked away to a helicopter hovering over the field and forest uplands of Roslea:

'People are being murdered every day.'

'*You* tell me that Sir . . . then I'll tell you . . . '

Harriet's nervous laugh came across the enclosure. She had been to the licensed tent before midday. Dinner would be awkward again this evening. He missed what George was saying, then heard:

'O'Donnell from the Show committee . . . he's one of them . . . and they're all like that . . . ' he clenched his fist, 'agin us.'

The Colonel looked into George's eyes. The fist gesture was both ridiculous and menacing. Aiden O'Donnell, a solitary Catholic on the Inver Show committee, was an English-schooled, week-end farmer, and a full-time barrister, his Jesuit brother on the teaching staff of Stonyhurst, another brother director with a Belfast merchant bank. O'Donnell had once said, 'I must argue for justice in a system I think unjust. Most of the time I feel hypocritical.' A disloyal statement? From a Northern Irish Catholic warmed by liberal wine, a predictable one. The Colonel understood both George's demand and O'Donnell's dilemma.

'George, you must understand . . . '

'O'Donnell goes or I quit . . . and you'll find another to shoe your horses.'

The Colonel shook his head. As he tried to find a

moderate reply, George turned and walked away. The Colonel watched him go. In comparison with such complexities war was a simple discipline, no weak links in the chain of command, deserters shot, the enemy destroyed, no confusing allegiances, no references to root causes, no twingings of conscience. In an unsubtle way George was right. O'Donnell had refused the bench. He would never truck with violence, but his ambivalence was as insidious as George's cast-iron bigotry, a subject in the old days for patrician table talk. 'Keep them hostile,' a powerful, landed neighbour had said with a bark-like chuckle, 'but not too hostile.' Now that this hostility had turned to rank hatred and daily murder, bigotry was no longer amusing. There seemed no solution. He moved towards the judges' stand. Alex was sitting on a low step of the platform, reading *The Belfast News Letter*, a cigar in his mouth; an ageing wrinkled primate in baggy suit, tartan shirt and horn-rimmed glasses, a hearing-aid clipped to his jacket. Harriet's ex-lover.

'Trouble, Nobby?'

'Nothing, where's Stuart?'

Alex pointed across the enclosure. Canon Plumm with rotund gravitas was talking to Professor Stuart Caldwell, the Canon gesticulating, Caldwell listening, the sun bright on his steel-framed glasses, a spare, almost boyish figure, clean and narrow as a sword. Alex folded the *News Letter* and thrust it into his jacket.

'It's the end, Nobby, the whole Show's folding . . . matter of months, less.'

'Saying that all your life Alex.'

'This time it really is, 'course I've nothing to lose, you stand to lose a lot.'

'Smallish crowd this year, not bad considering.'

'In the old days I used to sit up trees at night with

Basil watching out for Fenians or Germans . . . they never came . . . once I shot a rabbit . . . '

Alex paused. Unlistening, the Colonel scanned the grounds as Alex asked, 'Who's the enemy now, can you tell me that Nobby?'

'Harriet,' the Colonel said quietly. 'She's drinking a lot.'

A man with a silver trophy walked past leading a Charolais bull with a rosette on its forehead. He saluted the Colonel who said, 'Fine animal, Sam, well done.'

'Foreign, Sir, the ould breeds is dying out.'

'True.'

They watched the great golden bull pad towards a loading ramp.

'Never understood the cattle business,' Alex said. 'Lost a fortune trying to.'

The Colonel said again: 'Harriet, Alex, she's drinking a lot.'

Alex paused before saying: 'She dislikes the American.'

'Did she say so?'

'Can't you tell?'

Alex stood, brushing and blowing cigar ash from his jacket. 'Imagine spending eternity with old Plumm!'

'With anyone . . . can you speak to her?'

Alex shook his head. 'She's out of reach . . . and why die sober if you can afford to die drunk?'

'She's killing herself and you're facetious!'

'People get drunk to forget they're alive Nobby; happiness is under ground.'

The Colonel pondered this for a moment and said, with edge: 'That's heartless and rather stupid.'

As the Colonel moved to join the Canon and Caldwell, Alex muttered to himself: 'Suppose it is . . . but then I'm bankrupt every way.'

He took out another cigar and lit it. A group of farmers near by smiled indulgently. They could not hear what Alex muttered as he lit his cigar, but they knew he was Alex Boyd-Crawford, an oddity, something of a drinker and womaniser, a wise fool who would probably be the last of the Boyd-Crawfords, his estate depleted, a widower, his only son a drop-out, inheritor of one of the oldest names in Ulster.

Alex looked at his pocket-watch and muttered: 'Show's folding, time for a drink.'

He moved towards the marquee to extract Harriet without fuss.

'That,' he muttered, 'is one thing I can do better than Nobby.'

Leonard had driven about five miles on winding by-roads, through rolling drumlin countryside, up a dirt lane with high hedges to the front of a small two-storeyed farmhouse, painted tin over thatch, a byre adjoining, and beside it a small square concrete house with a rain-water tank above. There was a blue Cortina parked in an empty turf-shed.

'Where is this?' Lynam said.

'Mid-Monaghan. Townland of Drumgrone.'

'Is there a bathroom?'

He pointed to the small concrete building and said: 'A jacks.'

'Can I wash?'

'There's a tap in the back yard.'

She hesitated. Leonard added: 'There's a river at the bottom of the garden.'

'When do we leave?'

He looked at his wrist-watch: 'Eight-thirty.'

Leonard left her, went into the kitchen and directed his voice to someone behind the *Northern Standard*. 'Where are the boys?'

From behind the *Northern Standard* a voice said: 'Watching with Mother.'

'We have a guest, Jack.'

'Yes?'

The paper did not come down.

'She'll be at the river in five minutes or less . . . keep her in sight and stay out of sight.'

'She?'

'I'll tell you later; go out the back.'

Jack Gallagher went out the scullery door, round behind the barn, and keeping to the fields walked alongside the wild garden.

Lynam went to the concrete toilet, then round to a tap dripping into a sandstone trough. A scullery window looked directly out. She left the yard walking through the haggard, past an empty haybarn into an overgrown garden, dense with nettles, docks, and some kind of wild rhubarb, rank and gross-smelling, that reached the lower branches of a dozen tortured apple trees.

There was a trodden path from house to river. She could hear water. The bank was steeper than she expected, bracken fronds fringing both sides at the roots of alder, ash and thorn. Water flowed clear over the rust-coloured bed. She sat on a dry stone by the edge of the water, took out a small wash-bag, mirror and make-up. Wet from tension, the cool air felt good. When she took off her blouse she noticed damp sweat patches, and realised she was more frightened now than she had been on the silent journey from Dublin. In an hour or less she would be facing, maybe talking with, those two people she had seen in the show-ground, and very possibly present when they were shot. Round a table or from a platform it was easy to talk and propagate the merits of violence as she had done for two years. Different now that it had prowled to her side, the bloody mid-wife of regeneration, a ruthless animal with dripping mouth and glassy merciless eyes. She took off her sandals, put her feet and hands in the water. In the snug of a bar in Dorset Street, when she had told Burke how she had ended the pregnancy, the gravel-voiced arbiter of life and death was so stunned he could scarcely reply.

'Why do that?' he had asked.

'It had no future.'

'Why that?' he had repeated almost stupidly.

Was he so puerile that he saw her as a mere seed bed for his image? Why now without warning had he drafted her to possible martyrdom under Leonard? Pressures from others on the Army Council who disliked her bluntness? His wife's threat of suicide, or simply a cold, subtle move? Leonard, as yet publicly unknown, was privately spoken of North and South with a respect approaching awe which Burke must have noticed. And why had she joined? She tried to recall now her student impatience, bordering on hatred, for the congenital Irish condition, drunken meaningless talk breeding more drunken meaningless talk; an inability to think clearly and act coldly, 'like the British' Burke said with irony. Once in, men who seemed complex became common-place creatures jostling for power, a mix of waffling left-wingers, and old-fashioned Catholics led by Burke, who believed, she was certain, in nothing much but power for himself.

What now, sitting on a stone at a river's edge in Co. Monaghan, did she believe on this August evening? Aloud to the water she said: 'I don't know.'

Before Birmingham she could have walked across this river through a series of hump-backed fields to the nearest village, 'phoned a taxi, and caught the Larne ferry to oblivion, like others unsure, frightened, or disillusioned.

Somewhere up the river she heard the liquid bleat of a curlew. The gable of her grandmother's house faced the sea. At night the curlews swept up the stony inlet past Coolfada to Dungarvan. Coolfada, thatched roof roped against storm, mud floor, white-wash gone brown, smoke-yellowed glass, hens, dogs, cats, meal bags, a Pierce bellows and the leather-faced old woman, blood of her blood muttering Gaelic crossly to the animals, soda bread and sweet tea from a tin porringer in the morning, at night deep sleep in a settle bed in sheets stitched from flour bags, and God was the tide and all things related; people, fields, sea, sky, life and death, the immemorial land of childhood; lost.

It called again nearer. She looked up into the lowering sun as it winged closer. When she looked back to the river there was something floating downstream; rushes? a Moses' basket? The curlew wheeled calling again overhead and she thought 'I'm hallucinating'. Then she saw clearly a fawn shopping bag in rushwork design. It drifted past spinning in the shallows and on into a deep pool round the bend; plastic, illusive, childless. She had sacrificed the blood of her blood for what? A dream? Nothing, she thought, as fusty and narrow as nationalism or the dead sentimental drag of Coolfada. 'No,' she said aloud. She had chosen freely the waking nightmare of action, the comradeship of men whose vivid words, aims and violence seemed more attractive, honest and hopeful than the hollow crafty manoeuvrings of politicians like her father grinding out their mean, greedy lives towards anonymous death. For these reasons and others complex and unclear she had joined. Trapped now, frightened and betrayed, it was weak to say, 'I don't know', but thinking ahead she was not only sickened by violence but terrified at the idea of staring in its awful face. 'Oh God,' she muttered, but knowing she did not believe in God she accepted now her cowardice as natural. No option; she had chosen: so be it.

Dressed, she felt cool and fresh. She scrutinised her face in the small mirror. Who stared back? If she could fully understand the mind behind that mask she might begin to understand others a little and the world.

As she made up her face she became suddenly aware of something, a presence? She looked around sharply. Thirty yards downstream a young man was sitting at the edge of the river, his head just visible above the grass and bracken, a white fish-belly face that often goes with vivid red hair, no Monaghan farm boy. He was smiling and the effect was both attractive and repellent. She put the mirror away in her handbag, anger growing. How long had he been there? More shameful, more revealing that he should see her search in her mirror than see her wash. The soul more private than the body. Had he heard her speak aloud? He was moving towards her, still smiling, medium build, regulation jeans, polo, jerkin and desert boots.

'What are you grinning at?'

'Not much.'

'Did Leonard send you to watch?'

'You sound Dublin.'

'You sound pure Fermanagh.'

'Derry, love, and you're shivering . . . you'll catch your death.'

'Some day, and you?'

He was amused by her anger. 'Don't let on you're ashamed by a man's eyes; what do they call you?'

'*La belle dame sans merci.*'

The smile evaporated slowly; she waited for him to speak.

'I'm Jack Gallagher and I've notched five men in four years, three Brits, one R.U.C., one U.D.R., blown up three barracks, and left over a hundred bombs all over this province and when I ask a civil question I expect a civil answer.'

She smiled up at him and said:

'Je m'appelle Isabel Lynam, et je voudrais changer les choses telles qu'elles soient, sans des salopards comme toi, mais la cause a besoin de toi, comme les champs ont besoin du fumier des cochons.'

There was something in his expression that seemed almost subtle. She out-stared him, sure of her ground, till he turned and walked away from the river into the blind garden. Insulting and stupid of Leonard to have her watched like that. She picked up her handbag, momentarily aware that anger was more tolerable than fear, and that both were more tolerable than despair.

When Gallagher came into the yard Leonard could tell that he was tense.

'If I'm pig dung,' he said, 'she's sparrow shit. Bella Lynam, Christ man you're close, you could have warned me . . . why all the mystery . . . ?'

'You saw her?'

'And heard . . . smiling in my face she called me thug in French, that means you too boy, all of us.'

'I said to keep out of sight.'

'I was down river, she turned and saw me . . . is she with us tonight?'

Leonard nodded.

'She's suspect.'

'We're all suspect.'

When they heard Lynam padding up the yard, Leonard put a forefinger to his lips and made a small gesture commanding silence. When she came round the gable of the concrete toilet her face was inscrutable. Leonard smiled uneasily.

'Bella this is Jack Gallagher.'

'We've met,' Gallagher said without looking up.

She looked directly at Gallagher and said: 'Yes I know him.'

Leonard opened the door of the house to let her in. The kitchen was startling, green, white and gold boldly used on walls, ceiling and lino, gleaming formica-top table, chrome kitchen chairs with leatherette seats. Above the stove an enormous oleograph of the Sacred Heart, between a butcher's calendar and the two Johns, Kennedy and Roncali, framed in smiling profile. All other available shelf and wall space was taken up with clocks, grandmother, grandfather, a dozen wall clocks, wag-o-the-walls, cuckoo clocks, shelves of ticking alarm and marble, clocks from railway stations and reading rooms, and one very impressive piece cast in iron from a big house yard or stable. The room itself seemed a clicking mechanism. As she took this in she heard Leonard say:

'Pacelli.'

'Sorry?' she questioned.

Leonard repeated:

'Pacelli.'

'Pius the thirteenth,' Gallagher said.

A smallish youth approached her, a long almost monk-like face under crow black hair, with guileless eyes. A gunman? Incredulous, she took his hand as Leonard introduced her.

'Isabel Lynam.'

'Bella,' she said.

'We've heard plenty about you,' Pacelli said. The voice had a sharp Monaghan edge, and the smile was disconcerting, both mocking and reassuring; he was older than he appeared.

'Pacelli what?' she asked.

'McAleer,' he said.

'Touched like all the Monaghan McAleers,' Gallagher said.

'He means we believe in God, he lets on he doesn't.'

A replica of Pacelli came round the staircase and Pacelli said: 'This is Pascal the brother . . . Bella Lynam.'

As she shook hands she wondered if they were twins.

'How can I tell you apart?' she asked.

'Pascal has a bigger pendulum,' Gallagher said.

Leonard smiled and Pascal said: 'Jack's full of crack.'

'But sour like a crab.'

'Pay no heed.'

'Pass no remarks.'

'It's the kind of him.'

'He can't help it.'

'You'll get used to that,' Gallagher said. 'One goes tick the other goes tock.'

Pascal pointed a forefinger at Gallagher, cocked up his thumb, closed one eye and said: 'You'll mock once too often boy.'

'I leave that to God,' Gallagher said.

There was a short silence. It was clear to Lynam that the McAleer brothers did not approve of Gallagher's blasphemy. Seeing Gallagher close she noticed that his eyes were green, the whites blood-shot. His presence conveyed a tension you could almost touch. Because she knew he was a killer and enjoyed killing? Then Pascal said:

'You come on the express Bella?'

'By car.'

Pacelli smiled:

'The Boyne at Slane, Ardee in rain
    North to Carrickmacross
It's there the fields stare back and say
    Eternity will be no loss

'What do you think of our little hills?'

'Pleasing.'

'General Owen Roe marched through this townland in 1646.'

'He did?'

'Retreated half dead from syphilis,' Gallagher muttered.

'From what?' Pascal asked.

'Camp fever,' Leonard said.

'Lovers' plague, Pascal . . . won't bother you,' Gallagher explained.

'What's he at Martin?' Pacelli asked.

Leonard shrugged. 'We betray ourselves and are betrayed, and so we've lost time and again.'

'*Not* what I meant,' Gallagher said . . . 'Owen Roe tried and lost . . . we'll win or die trying.'

'Fair enough,' Pascal said.

'I'm with you there,' Pacelli added.

Gallagher looked at Lynam. 'What do you say Mademoiselle?'

For five seconds Lynam stared back, before saying: 'Little men who sneer at giants are ludicrous.'

Leonard turned away so that Gallagher would not see him smile. Pascal aware of increasing tension intervened backed by Pacelli.

'The Mammy wants to meet you.'

'She's above in the bed.'

'An invalid.'

'Bed-ridden this five years, arthritis and a dose of other things.'

'She'll tell you herself.'

'Likes to talk.'

Leonard indicated to Lynam that she would have to do as requested. She followed Pascal across the gleaming green lino then up the narrow staircase. He opened a bedroom door.

'Bella Lynam from Dublin, Mammy, you've heerd tell of her.'

A deep woman's voice uttered something in the room. Pascal smiled as she went in, closing himself out. Mrs McAleer was enormous, an Irish Queen Victoria, with de Valera's nose and Churchill's mouth, all chin and breast, her stomach making a tent of the patchwork quilt, plaited hair bunned up behind, and lenses so powerful that her eyes peered out in huge and permanent astonishment. She looked as though she could deliver Pascal and Pacelli fully grown. As Lynam approached Mrs McAleer held out a plump, regal hand. Lynam took it. It was clammy, the arthritic fingers rigid. The room had a personal fishy smell, mixed with Lysol and deodorant. Above a bedside commode a frail madonna stared upwards in tears, her heart transfixed by a sword. Beside the madonna, a calendar print of Padraig Pearse, his head in a halo of flames. Underneath someone had printed in red biro, his poem, 'The Mother'. Mrs McAleer said:

'You don't look twenty, I thought you'd be older.'

'I feel like a thousand.'

'You'll be with them tonight?'

'Yes.'

'Are you afraid daughter?'

'Of course.'

'It's a joy we can still breed your likes.'

The fishmonger smell was oppressive. Lynam moved to a partially opened window and looked at the August landscape and the evening. Mrs McAleer patted the patchwork quilt and said:

'You can sit here by me.'

'The view is beautiful,' Lynam said.

'It is, it is, a wonder and a pity when you think of the men and women who died for them crooked hedges, ditches and lanes, the blood, the hunger, the burials, the old sorrow. I've suffered too all my life. Hughie my husband, that's him in the snap, used to say to me, "Listen Rosie don't argue with God's will, he knows best," a religious man, a feeling man, couldn't get doctors enough for me, London, Belfast, Dublin, no solution. They got him in '57 with a gun near Armagh, tortured and locked him away five years, then let him out to die. In this his deathbed he said to the boys, "I'm broke lads, finished, but you have a score to settle," and them only half reared, and me half crippled. Sometimes I think life's a bigger tragedy nor death. The Dublin Doctor Fagan said to me "Mrs McAleer," he said, "there's nothing for it only aspirins and patience." To myself I thought, "Patience unto death".'

She paused to take a breath and change gear. 'What do you think of my boys, daughter?'

'They seem nice.'

'Small, like Hugh, but big hearts and clean living, and they've got nerve, don't smoke, don't drink, don't interfere with girls like that Gallagher, and they can take down any clock in the world and put it up again, and bombs . . . ! Not a one in this country to touch them . . . Mr Burke told me himself, "You should be proud Mrs McAleer, proud, they'll get their reward and so will you." Every day I thank God for my three green fields and my two brave sons.'

She sighed. Lynam was about to say something when Mrs McAleer continued:

'I was once a slip of a girl like you would you believe that? And look at me now. Only for my two boys I'd be lost entirely, and I could lose them any time, some day, some night, like tonight, they'll go off, and the neighbour woman that cares me will come in some morning and say: "I'm afeered Mrs McAleer I've bad news for you," and I'll say: "My boys is it, both?" And she'll nod.'

Mrs McAleer bowed her head and quoted:

'Lord thou art hard on mothers,
We suffer in their coming and their going,
And though I grudge them not, I weary, weary
Of the long sorrow, and yet I have my joy,
My sons were faithful and they fought.'

Mrs McAleer looked up. 'I wouldn't be the first nor the last, it's the price of freedom; you're too young to understand the dread, your own flesh and blood dead in the cold earth.'

'I understand.'

'Young girls like you shouldn't be in danger . . . war is men's work, if them Brits or black Protestants got hands on you, you'd never stand up to them . . . what made you join, daughter?'

'That you wouldn't understand.'

'Why not?'

'Because . . . ' Lynam paused, aware of the great devouring eyes, and said: 'I don't understand myself.'

'To free Ireland, it's simple.'

'For what?'

'Us.'

'From what?'

'Them.'

'We are them . . . now.'

The blancmange cheeks trembled till the mouth uttered: 'Never . . . despise us, always did, always will.'

From the window Lynam saw Gallagher cross the yard and place a canvas bag in the boot of the blue

Cortina. She said quietly: 'We died long ago with our language.'

'What are you saying girl?'

'Win or lose nothing changes, because men don't nor women . . . even the blind know that light leads on to darkness.'

In the silence that followed, they could hear the ticking of innumerable clocks from the kitchen below. Mrs McAleer opened her mouth to say something, hesitated, then said, almost tenderly:

'You sound honest, do you pray daughter?'

'When I'm frightened.'

'Do you believe in God?'

'Not yours.'

'Jesus Christ?'

'Not yours.'

The great face darkened again. On the edge of anger she said loudly. 'There's only one Jesus Christ.'

'Dozens Mrs Mac., and they hate each other.'

There was a heavy silence punctuated by a sudden storm of cuckoo clocks and a dozen reverberating gongs in the kitchen.

'Are you a Communist, child?'

'I'm twenty-three. Arts graduate, only child of Willie Lynam, publican, Dáil Deputy and drunkard, separated from his wife, my mother, who devotes herself to poodles and Jesuits, and soon I will be in jail, exiled or dead.'

Lynam paused and turned from the window. 'What I am or think doesn't matter, but I'm glad we've met.'

In silence Mrs McAleer pointed a crooked finger to a chest of drawers facing the bed.

'Left-hand drawer, open it.'

Lynam did as she was asked. There was a cardboard box, a large plastic bottle and dozens of empty aspirin bottles filled with transparent liquid.

'Open the box.'

Lynam took off the cardboard lid and saw a hoard of miraculous medals and chains.

'Take one and a small bottle.'

Lynam felt absurd but knew refusal would give serious offence.

'Here daughter . . . sit.'

Mrs McAleer put the medal over Lynam's head and poked it under her blouse. Lynam slipped the aspirin bottle into her bag.

'You know what that is?'

'Holy water?'

'Better again, Lourdes water; she believes in you girl, and you mind that.'

Mrs McAleer was holding her with a crab-like grip between rigid thumb and forefinger. Close up the two great floating eyes in that flaccid face had the impact of a Hogarth cartoon.

'Always wanted a daughter . . . if I had one she wouldn't be troubled like you . . . too much learnin' is the ruination of the world, all a body needs is faith in God, his Blessed Mother, faith in your people and faith in your country.'

'Goodbye Mrs McAleer.'

'God go with you child.'

Lynam closed the door quietly and stood dazed in the narrow upstairs hall. Mrs McAleer was a rural, Republican edition of her genteel mother who fed anzaks and coffee to rotating Jesuits in return for vapid spiritual consolation. In every part of this island she had met men and women unreal beyond description. A race of inbred lunatics? Sometimes it seemed frighteningly like that.

She could hear Leonard talking below. When she rounded the bottom of the staircase he had his finger on a map or drawing. As she moved towards the table Gallagher came in the front door his cold face fixed in amused contempt. Without irony Pascal asked:

'You got your medal Bella?'

'Yes.'

And Pacelli added: 'Your wee bottle?'

Lynam nodded.

'Pre-war,' Gallagher said. 'Drink it and you'll get typhoid.'

Pascal and Pacelli said almost together:

'Don't mind him.'

'He's bred that way.'

Gallagher smiled and said: 'Tick tock, tick tock.'

'Can we keep to this?' Leonard asked, his finger on a drawing. To Lynam he added: 'You'll be with me, I'll gen you up on the way.'

'Can I come and watch?' Gallagher asked.

For a moment it seemed as though Leonard would reply. It was Pacelli who spoke. 'No call for talk like that.'

'Like what?'

'Bad talk,' Pacelli said.

'What the fuck did I say?'

Lynam moved away. In the silence that followed she read the legend on a butcher's calendar her back to the table. Pascal said:

'That's too much, no man should talk like that fornenst wemen.'

'She doesn't give a shit about you boy, me, any of us.'

'You can tell?' Leonard asked.

'I can tell,' Gallagher said.

Her back to them Lynam said: 'Let him fuck all he likes if it makes him feel manly.'

'Not you,' Gallagher said. 'I don't pick over garbage.'

The McAleer brothers were very uncomfortable. Leonard said quietly: 'Jack please.'

Lynam looked around. Leonard was white. A nerve twitched under his blind eye. She looked at the green lino aware of a sudden release of adrenalin. As always when tense she smiled. In the silence that followed the clocks seemed suddenly hysterical. Without opening his mouth Gallagher said:

'Bloody women, muck everything.'

Leonard was aware that this was mostly his fault. Burke's cryptic coded note had advised him to watch her. The river thing was unfortunate. Either of the McAleers would have been more discreet, and Gallagher would have been more careful had he known who she was. To Gallagher all females were for screwing in ditches or cars. He boasted his prowess as lover and killer, how the girls whimpered, how his targets spun, stumbled and fell, date, street, and townland, all carefully reported back to Dublin: History. An epileptic, a sick aura of success hung about him, the black flag of violence and death. In the further silence Leonard looked from face to face, Gallagher's rigid, the McAleer brothers' aware of unseemliness. Lynam kept her head bowed. Was she smiling? With emphasis now he said:

'That's it.'

'Come off it Martin.'

Gallagher pointed a trigger finger at Lynam. 'We know about her, Bella Donna, Burke calls her, she's poisonous, maybe Special Branch, Dublin or London, both the one . . . you're doing the Belfast gent and she's laughing at you . . . all of us . . . look at her, we're a joke.'

They all looked at Lynam. She lifted her head and stared back, her face indecipherable. Leonard paused for control. As he was about to speak a bell sounded upstairs.

'Mother Lourdes on the line,' Gallagher said.

Both McAleers moved for the staircase. Leonard looked at his watch.

'Five minutes, boys, make your farewells . . . ' To Gallagher he said: 'You'd better say your bit and be done with this.'

Gallagher said: 'Thios ansin ag an abhainn thug tu cailleach orm sul a rachaimid ait ar bit anois gabhfaidh tu mo leath sgeala.'*

Lynam was startled. In the silence which followed a faint colour came into her narrow cheek bones. She said, nodding towards Leonard: 'I was angry with him not you.'

'Mea culpa, it was stupid of me.'

'I'll drink to that,' Gallagher said, and moved towards a cupboard beside the range. He took out a bottle of Powers Gold Label and half-filled three plain tumblers. He topped up with water from a jug, handed a glass to Leonard and Lynam, raised his own and said:

'To Ireland free.'

'Whatever that means,' Lynam muttered.

Gallagher lowered his tumbler. 'From the centre to the sea, girl, that's what it means.' He paused, looking intently into her face, and said: 'And no deals, no compromise ever, no Catholic gents on horseback telling us what to think, no Murphys in a wig locking us away because they're afraid, no po-faced Prods whipping us for white nigger trash, no smug clergy hiding behind props and property, and whining about violence, no jet-set, pin-stripes buying up half the country; that's what

*'Down at the river you called me a thug . . . before we go anywhere you'll apologise.'

125

it means Lynam.' He jiggled his glass. 'And death to all traitors . . . you'll drink to that? . . . '

'I'll drink to that.'

'You believe it?'

'I'll drink to it.'

She was startled, not so much by what he said but by the articulate intensity, the twisting mouth and bloodshot eyes, the low key fury as words came jerking out with barely controlled violence . . . Had she misjudged him at the river as a boastful moron? This he was, but more. Could Leonard, anyone, control such a creature. The cold whiskey burned its way down, spreading a warm blurring numbness in her empty stomach. I'll be drunk in five minutes she thought, maybe dead by Monday. Gallagher added now:

'And success to the job.'

'I'll be big,' Leonard said, raising his glass and lowering his voice. 'The world,' he said, 'and the socialist future.'

'Does it have one?' Lynam asked.

'Can you let nothing by?' Gallagher asked.

'What the fight's about partly,' Leonard intervened.

They drank and Gallagher looked at Lynam. 'Now your dream?'

There was quite a pause till she said with an odd smile: 'Life and death.'

They hesitated.

'Whose death?' Gallagher asked.

'Peace,' she said.

'That's better,' Leonard said, and realised that she knew clearly as he did what they were venturing . . . Two Army Council meetings had been, he was told, entirely taken up with 'The Inver Move'. The first vote went against, the second in favour. He had spent three long days and sleepless nights being briefed in Dublin. At the time Burke had said that he might send extra help, but had given him no hint that it would be Lynam. Since then Leonard had thought of nothing else night and day, trying to justify in advance, to cancel fear and doubt. The wealth and privilege of the Armstrongs in these islands and Europe had been gained by force and fraud, sanctioned and maintained by Church and Law for centuries. This he told himself again and again. If London refused to negotiate they would have to kill and be killed. The clamorous condemnations that would follow were nothing; they would be at peace. He had shot one soldier near Strabane two years ago and one bomb he had placed had killed a mother and child. It was painful to see images in newspapers and read accounts. Sometimes he heard screaming in his sleep and woke sweating. Unlike Gallagher he had never seen, nor wanted to, the face of a victim. This time they would be face to face in one room for eighteen hours or more. As the McAleers came down the staircase Leonard asked:

'Time?'

Pascal and Pacelli looked at their wrist-watches, smiled at the clocks round the walls and said:

'Eight twenty-five.'

'Dead on.'

Gallagher and Leonard adjusted their watches fractionally and Leonard said: 'We leave in five minutes.'

Pascal and Pacelli came up to Leonard and shook his hand in solemn ritual. They then turned to Lynam. She was about to offer her hand when Pascal kissed her on one cheek, Pacelli on the other. Both had the same joyous, guileful smiles, at variance with their guileless eyes. Gallagher watched them go out the door, followed, turned and said:

'Slán.'

'Slán,' Leonard and Lynam said simultaneously.

'Have they killed?' she asked.

'Yes.'

'Both?'

'Yes.'

'And you?'

'Yes.'

'All but me.'

'You might have to.'

'I know.'

'You have a weapon?'

'No.'

Leonard put his glass down. She noticed he had scarcely touched it. He went to the built-in cupboard where Gallagher had found the whiskey, took out two shelves, removed a loose board from the back and put his hand into a cavity. He took out a small pistol.

As he explained how it worked his voice seemed far away. She could see his scarred thumb pressing the catch, his forefinger curling round the trigger: then words: 'Dead simple, safety catch, gentle pressure, flick this here, can't miss, hold the shooting wrist with your hand, like this.' Gallagher's measure of whiskey seemed to heighten the gleaming phallic awfulness in Leonard's hands. He undid the catch of her bag, and thrust in the pistol. If he had unzipped his fly, peeled off a used condom and dropped it in her bag, she would have been less shocked. He was aware of her silence.

'All right?'

'Fine.'

As he held the front door open he called out: 'Monday night late Mrs Mac.'

The deep voice above sent down a sepulchral blessing.

The Cortina went first, Pascal driving, Gallagher in front, Pacelli in the back. After ten minutes scudding along a by-road into the gathering dusk they passed a sign which said: 'UNAPPROVED ROAD'.

From the back seat Pacelli grinned and gave the thumbs up sign. Leonard nodded and thumbed back at him.

'This is it,' he said.

Lynam did not answer. After a mile she said: 'We're dead.'

'Every time I think that and I'm still alive.'

'This is different.'

'More difficult . . . if it wasn't it wouldn't be worth doing.'

'Suppose we're stopped on the way by police or Army?'

'We won't be.'

'Suppose?'

'This road's checked out, and all by-roads.'

'How?'

'Friends.'

The Cortina slowed, turned left up a by-road; as Leonard slowed to follow he said: 'Clumsy . . . the river thing, I'm sorry.'

Lynam said nothing for a minute, then asked: 'Where did he get French?'

'Brittany, Breton Freedom Fighter.'

'Will he do what you say?'

'Jack? I think so.'

'Think?'

'I'm sure.'

'He's paranoid, schizoid.'

'Epileptic.'

'I could sense something, the sick colour and the raving.'

'If it comes to killing he won't waste words.'

'Or pity?'

'No,' Leonard said, 'he's dedicated and deadly.'

'What did Burke tell you?'

'If it was serious you wouldn't be here.'

'Tell me.'

Leonard hesitated before saying: 'Anyone who can wreck two marriages and arrange three press leaks in one year should be in advertising or a brothel.'

'He's lying . . . reptile.'

'All of us, if you believe the Press, Churches and politicians.'

In a few sentences Leonard outlined what she would have to do. He asked if she was clear. She said yes she was. They were now in forest twilight away from the small drumlin fields with their ditches of thorn and thwarted ash. They sped past a limestone baronial gate-lodge with conifers crowding and stretching back into the embracing dark. A hundred yards further on there was an obelisk in a circular clearing, its base engraved in gold lettering. Leonard said, nodding at it:

'The dead of two world wars.'

'Is this Inver?'

Leonard nodded. The Cortina had stopped a hundred yards from the monument where the high estate wall had been smashed by a falling tree. Gallagher and Pascal had gone through. Pacelli took the canvas bag from the boot and followed. Leonard drew in behind the Cortina and cut his engine. As Lynam stepped over the rubble of the wall she saw below a long stretch of lake and meadowland and, beyond the lake, bunched in trees and shrubbery, the outline of a tall Tudor house.

Millicent left the tray on the pantry table, plugged in the coffee percolator and watched her father decanting port, waiting for him to say something.

'I've spoken to her.'

'When?'

'Before dinner.'

The Colonel inserted a cork firmly into the empty bottle of port as his daughter said: 'Her blouse is buttoned the wrong way, and out at the back, and she's been like a zombie all through dinner.'

'Worse when she talks.'

'It's awful to say this, father, but I'll leave on Monday if she doesn't . . . I can understand today at the Show, but other days where does she get it?'

'The staff are "loyal".'

'Why is she so unhappy?'

'Why does winter come?'

'She fell in the marquee when Alex went to . . .'

'Yes I heard.'

'Such a mockery of a man.'

'He's kindly, reads a lot, they share that.'

'Don't you care?'

The Colonel had moved towards the heavy, panelled

self-closing door that gave to the living-room. If he said yes it would be short of honest. No, and it would seem that he did not love or cherish his wife, her mother, when in truth he had connived at the affair through guilt. He looked at the decanter of port and said:

'Yes and no.'

'That's not an answer.'

'The best I can give.'

Because they were only six the hunting table was opened before the Adam grate in the long high-ceilinged living-room cleared now except for two ashtrays, port glasses, and some cut-glass tumblers. Harriet was sitting at the head of the table facing the high, wide, bay window that looked south-west across the lake. All through dinner she had been watching a dark red sun go down behind the forest lands of Inver and Shannock, leaving the lake a blooded gash in the quiet landscape. Now, as she watched, the blood congealed to a blackish, navy-blue, as lake, field and forest merged into night.

Caldwell had been talking and getting attention through dinner. Harriet lit her last cigarette watching the moving lips, hating the intelligent blue eyes behind those steel frames, the sickening drawl, the elegant brown safari-type jacket, and creamy silk shirt that seemed to blend with his feminine skin. Alex was nodding, bored, she thought. Canon Plumm seemed attentive. Suddenly the Canon's face broadened. He gave a short avuncular laugh. Caldwell smiling touched the tip of his fine-boned nose with a long left forefinger. Harriet noticed the perfectly groomed nails. Some rhyming joke? She had missed it. In the momentary pause that followed she said with unusual loudness:

'Very stupid of me but I seem to have missed the point.'

The Colonel was at the other end of the table. As he

sat and placed the decanter of port he said with quiet hardness: 'Possibly you weren't listening my love.'

Caldwell said: 'It's nothing.'

'But Canon Plumm laughed,' Harriet said. 'It must be amusing.'

There was a longer pause. Harriet looked from face to face and then began:

'Sitting snugly at his fire William Wordsworth said to Charles Lamb, "I could write plays like Shakespeare if I'd a mind to," and Lamb replied, "Nothing lacking Willie, but the mind".'

Alex Boyd-Crawford smiled; he had heard it before. No one else responded. Harriet went on:

'Oscar Wilde envied that reply, did you know that Professor?'

'I did not.'

'Shy man Lamb, devoted to his sister, charming essays.'

Harriet could see the knuckles of her husband's hands go white as both fists closed. Surely he wasn't going to bang the table? She kept her eyes down and heard Caldwell say:

'More sick than funny I suppose.'

'What?' Harriet asked.

Canon Plumm explained. 'Professor Caldwell was telling us about some grave inscriptions in eighteenth-century Virginia.'

'Which Virginia?'

'United States.'

'Grave inscriptions?'

'Yes.'

'Funny ones, Professor?'

'Odd ones,' Caldwell said.

'In our graveyard here,' Canon Plumm ventured, when Harriet cut in suddenly.

'Hideous subject, utterly.'

She searched the ornate Italian frieze for a word, found it and uttered emphatically:

'Horrendous . . . numbing . . . if you ponder it . . . thy kingdom dumb . . . terrifying . . . ' She paused. 'But life itself, now there's true comedy, because people do the strangest, the most anguish-making, cruelly funny things . . . friends, neighbours, nations . . . when I think of the things we all do to each other in the course of living, in the mill of history, I laugh and laugh till the tears come.'

Harriet bowed her head. She was trembling, forgot what she was saying and why, aware only that Milly had placed a tray with coffee cups and percolator on the table and was now sitting down.

'What was I saying Alex?'

'Something about life dear.'

'Ah yes, some burial joke that Dr Caldwell made . . . I missed the point, and that is a defect, not to respond to the niceties of civilised necrophilia.'

The Colonel said coldly: 'Harriet.'

'Yes my love?'

'Would you like to pour coffee?'

'I'll pour,' Millicent said.

They watched as she poured, each responding when she asked about sugar and cream.

'Some graves,' Alex said vaguely, 'are self-dug.'

'Indeed,' the Colonel said, looking directly at his wife. Behind those eyes, she thought, a mind foreign as his locked study. The charm was for others, that tilt of the head as though he could listen for ever. Long since he had stopped hearing unless she screamed. What had she loved or thought she loved? The soldierly bearing, the graceful manners, the family accumulations, in Tudor mellowness. He knew about everything in the house, who bought it, where, when, why, how much it was insured for. Yes. He understood about insurance. 'Any policy, Nobby, for a withering heart?' He had smiled that night as though she had asked a silly question, the smile he used when talking with her gifted unpredictable father whose money had helped finance the expensive yards, the milking merry-go-round, the yards full of cows and bawling bullocks. Some time near dawn she had smashed three plates of value against the door of his study. He did not refer to the gesture at the time or since. The armour of infinite politeness, behind it something callous; inhuman.

Aloud she said, 'Inhuman.'

No one seemed to hear. The talk now had shifted to employment, the E.E.C. and agriculture. Agriculture. His real devotion since the war; his hobbies, military and local history: 'The Armstrongs in Ulster: The intruders who contributed.'

In the functions room of an Armagh hotel his paper was well received by the Clogher Historical Society, Catholics and Protestants, mostly teachers and clergy. She had read it in advance and thought it dull and tendentious. When he spoke it standing upright in that warm level voice, it sounded humane, conscientious, liberal. Everyone likes him for some reason, she thought . . . perhaps I'm jealous . . . Yes. All that correspondence with Denis Brogan which she had resented till they met at Cambridge, an Irish-Scot professor, with a port-wine face, startling white hair, and a mind so complex and comprehensive that his tongue stumbled after, a soul more alive to poetry and philosophy, than the brutal facts and farce of war. In comparison Caldwell was an intellectual eunuch, a beautiful, polished New England eunuch. She was aware now that they were all looking at Alex. Watching his pursed mouth she forced herself to understand what he was saying. He paused, shrugged and continued:

'We never employed Papists, family tradition, they all cheat, lie and thieve, dirty, careless, superstitious, stupid; when you hear this from the nursery onwards, right or wrong it tends to stick.'

'Fact, Sir,' Canon Plumm said gravely. 'They've a lower I.Q. than Negroes, an American professor has proven this, am I right Dr Caldwell?'

Caldwell considered a moment and said: 'That study is controversial, Canon.'

'To the Irish, no one else; what they've done down there in sixty years is not in doubt, ruined Dublin, painted pillar boxes green, and produced more lunatics and alcoholics per square mile than any other country in the world. This is proven fact.'

Harriet finished her glass of wine, wiped her mouth with a napkin.

'Did you not say, Milly, that this lovely county of ours has the worst housing problem in these islands?'

'It has,' Millicent said.

'Papist housing you'll find,' the Canon said, 'won't avail of grants, they're shiftless and Rome's responsible.'

'Rome?' Harriet asked.

The Canon smiled and shook his head patiently as he muttered: 'Italy, Spain, Portugal, Latin America.'

He opened his hands and pursed his lips. The target was so enormous he did not know quite where to aim. Suddenly he struck. 'Take Plunkett, the rebel priest, hung as Crown traitor. This year they plan to canonise him.'

He paused, staring from face to face. 'Here their Bishops preach against violence while the Pope in Rome aligns himself with I.R.A. bombers and murderers.'

He paused again. 'This is not just mischievous; it's political, criminal.'

There was an embarrassed pause, until Harriet said: 'We did burn Joan of Arc, Canon . . . they made her a saint.'

'Different.'

'Is it? Of course I don't understand politics; Nobby does and Professor Caldwell is an expert. How does it strike you, Professor, as an outsider? Will we be shot in our beds, driven to the sea, what's your impression?'

'Do you want an answer?'

'I did ask a question.'

'Unlikely . . . implausible.'

'Then what is plausible?'

Stuart Caldwell stirred his coffee for ten seconds, aware that no reply could please.

'I expect,' he said quietly, 'the British will leave in time, and North and South will patch up something in time, with or without a civil war . . . impossible to say more.'

Almost inaudibly Harriet muttered: 'Profound.'

Glacial, the Colonel asked: 'You have some solution, dear?'

'No, but I did think the Canon just now sounded peasant as Paisley without the loudmouthed charm, and I don't trust his American professor I.Q. expert, or indeed anything from that glorious civilisation.'

'Mother.'

'You've got a degree dear, what did they teach you at Trinity? To keep silent when people talk nonsense?'

Harriet looked down the table at her husband. Centuries of arrogance in those bloodhound eyes that stared back from that long hawk-like face drained of colour, the iron grey head and clipped moustache fringing a heavy mouth. She looked away to the window across the lake.

The Colonel looked up at his wife who was avoiding his eyes. Last night she had fallen asleep at table. He had excused the staff and helped Milly serve dinner to eight people. Her performance this evening was a great deal more painful. Of course John Plumm was something of a bigot and a bore, but also well-meaning in his way, apart from being a very old friend. Stuart was much too sophisticated to respond to drunken petulance. Tomorrow when she half remembered what she had just said she would suffer. He felt both angry with her and sorry for her.

Harriet stood suddenly and walked with particular care towards the pantry door. In the continuing silence Alex said:

'Excellent coffee . . . excellent.'

'It is,' Caldwell said.

The Colonel stood and said to Canon Plumm and Caldwell: 'I'm sorry.'

The Canon shook his head and mumbled something. Caldwell smiled and made a small gesture. The Colonel followed Harriet. She was standing at the sink with a large whiskey looking out at the August night. The Colonel approached quietly, held her wrist, took the glass from her hand and moved to the table. She watched with anger and disbelief as he poured the whiskey back into a newly-opened bottle of Haig then heard herself say:

'That was a stupid thing to do.'

'You've been warned my love . . . you're killing yourself.'

'I'm dead.'

'Drunk, dear, and the trouble is you'll fall and crack your skull or crash the car.'

'A blessed relief.'

The Colonel looked at the label on the whiskey bottle and said: 'Irish is cheaper than Scotch and better for making you drunk. If you get more . . . '

'A blessed relief, I said. And you will not humiliate me like this.'

The Colonel watched, impassive, a seasoned politician pausing for an irrelevant heckler. Looking from the scrubbed deal table to her glazed brown eyes he said with growing edge:

'If you get more maudlin than you are now, insult guests like that, laugh hysterically at nothing, or jabber incomprehensible verse, I'll send for someone.'

He had hinted before; now it had been said. She felt anger grow to a point of fury.

'Someone!'

'Qualified.'

She turned her back and said to the window: 'Get a medical plumber for me, Nobby, and I'll 'phone someone for you . . . also qualified.'

There was a very long pause before the Colonel said: 'What are you trying to say my love?'

'I can see through him with my eyes shut.'

'Who?'

'Caldwell.'

'You dislike him?'

'He makes me ill, I want him gone.'

'You could have said so without all this.'

The Colonel went back to the living-room. Harriet leaned against the pantry sink supporting herself with both hands. The table before her seemed momentarily a raft riding on a gentle swell. She closed her eyes aware that the door leading off the pantry to the kitchen corridor had opened quietly, or had she imagined it? She opened her eyes and saw a young man with blood red hair above a corpse white face. He was pointing a pistol at her. He waved her away from the sink. More incredulous than afraid she moved as directed towards the table and thought to herself: I'm dreaming. The young man locked the door, moved across the pantry, locked another door leading to the hall, went to the sink, pulled the shutters across the window, then the curtains, and pointed towards the door leading into the living-room. As she opened this green baize door she saw another young man, tall with a black beard, standing with a pistol at the far end of the room, beside him a girl with a tense narrow face, and melancholy eyes. The girl had no weapon in her hand. The man with the beard spoke.

'No hardship intended if our request is met.'

The red youth walked down the long room, pulled shutters across the bay window, then the heavy tapestry curtains, ensuring that there was no gap in the middle or at either side.

The family portraits round the walls looked calmly down on the upturned faces round the hunting table, each face expressing varying degrees of incomprehension and disbelief. The Tomkin clock on the high mantel ticked evenly in the stillness that followed Leonard's cryptic statement, beech logs hissed in the Adam fire-basket. Lynam looking from face to face was startled by a sudden shock of recognition: 'No . . . ! Yes . . . ? Trinity . . . ? Armstrong . . . ? Good Christ . . . !' They had shared French tutorials three years ago. She could see that the Armstrong girl could not believe the evidence of her own eyes. To Lynam she said:

'It is you?'

'Yes,' Lynam said.

High in the great house they could hear shutters squealing on rusty hinges, the rasp of iron clasps, the twanging of six-inch nails being driven into doors, architraves, windows.

Leonard switched on the lights.

'How many?' the Colonel asked.

'Two more.'

'How long will you keep us?'

'Tomorrow midday, unless they give us what we ask.'

'And that is?'

'Three men from Long Kesh.'

'And if not?'

'Bleak . . . for all of us.'

Gallagher approached and whispered, nodding towards the table:

'Milord Secretary . . . he's gone . . . !'

'We'll make these do.'

'Bad start.'

'Good omen.'

Watching them the Colonel guessed the content and spoke:

'You know that what you're attempting is not just misguided, it's plain stupid.'

The red-haired youth made a brief grimace. The man with the beard, obviously the leader, returned the Colonel's stare. His left eye was sunken in its socket, both heavy-lidded above a prow-like nose, the dense beard creating a mask-like effect. Having spoken, the Colonel now felt he had to act. He stood, not quite knowing what he intended, and moved towards Leonard. With scarcely a movement of lips a voice came from the beard with emphasis:

'No further.'

The scarred forefinger of his left hand was pointing rigidly. The effect was more menacing than a pistol. Some instinct advised the Colonel that this man was professional and would kill without hesitation. He paused, looked at the decanter of port on the table and said:

'You expected my son-in-law here . . . he's chairing a symposium at Queen's University. I would have thought you knew this – it was well publicised. You can't bargain with an old soldier, his family and a couple of friends – won't work. You'll have to kill us – they'll kill you – and nothing whatever will have been gained but bad propaganda for you and more business for the undertakers, and God knows they're overworked in this Province . . . Be sensible . . . you can still leave.'

'Your Army is notified,' Leonard said. 'On its way.'

'If they don't get lost about Belturbet,' Gallagher muttered.

'Dear God,' Canon Plumm almost whispered.

'I think,' the Colonel said, 'that you should know this gentleman is an American professor.'

Gallagher said: 'He could be an Australian kangaroo.'

Leonard nodded agreement. 'He's here and stays till we decide . . . otherwise, no hardship. The house will be sealed excepting the front door and hall, this room, the pantry and toilet off.'

The Colonel said: 'You know the house well.'

'National Trust,' Leonard said. 'The plans are available and clear.'

Harriet looked at her husband as the nailing continued above. 'We're being entombed, Nobby, alive.'

Milly said: 'Mother, I think . . . '

'We can talk, can we not?'

'All you like,' Leonard said.

'Then I think we should introduce ourselves.'

In the silence that followed Leonard said: 'Our names don't matter.'

'Ours do . . . I am Harriet Armstrong and that is my husband Norbert, beside him is Stuart Caldwell, a Pro-

142

fessor of military history . . . a subject indistinguishable from pornography in my view . . . I read a lot of poetry . . . Dylan Thomas mostly.'

Milly said: 'Mother this is not helpful.'

Leonard said: 'I'm quite interested.'

'In mockery,' Millicent said acidly.

'I said "Quite".'

Harriet went on: 'The Professor probably knows more about the I.R.A. than any of you people.'

'I doubt it,' Gallagher said.

'And this,' she said, putting out her hand towards Alex, 'is Alex Boyd-Crawford retired from . . . what are you retired from Alex?'

'Everything,' Alex said.

'But genial courtesy and warmth . . . human warmth . . . rare in this cold world . . . and beside me this roundabout man is dear Canon Plumm, the Rector of Inver Church . . . an expert on bee-keeping.' She paused and smiled before adding: 'And the machinations of the Vatican . . . And my daughter Millicent, twenty-four years old . . . married . . .'

'Harriet you will stop talking now,' the Colonel's voice cracked out in hard sharp command.

Harriet shrugged, picked up an empty cigarette carton, examined it, turned to Gallagher and asked: 'Do you have a cigarette?'

Without answering Gallagher produced a packet with his free hand and flicked it on to the table.

'Thank you.'

As Harriet lit a cigarette, Gallagher studied the six faces round the table, then moved away and began pacing the length of the room, pausing once or twice before family portraits, glancing into the great gilt mirror above the chimneypiece which framed the hostages round the table, now looking into each others' eyes like passengers aboard plane or ship when an engine bursts into flame, or a voice warns suddenly of serious emergency. The man with the beard, who was obviously the leader, seemed almost casual, talking in a low voice with the girl. The red youth seemed very tense and by far the most dangerous. Every now and then his pistol wrist gave an involuntary twitch like the tail of a caged tiger.

Watching him Lynam realised with slow horror that he would convey this tension till he had tasted blood. He wanted to kill or be killed, and she wondered if this, less manifest, was a hidden instinct in herself, in Leonard, in the McAleers. Then she saw the Colonel lean over the back of the American's chair and say something to his daughter who asked:

'Can I fetch some whiskey?'

'Where from?'

'The pantry.'

Leonard nodded and said quietly to Lynam: 'Go with her.'

Millicent got up. Lynam followed and stood in the panelled pantry beside a Welsh dresser decked with Spode china, Wedgwood, oriental ware, and topped with an array of pewter mugs and containers. Millicent hunkered, reached into a corner cupboard and took out two bottles of Bushmills whiskey aware that Lynam was standing behind her. She straightened, turned, and said:

'When I heard your voice I knew . . . Isabel Lynam?'

'Yes.'

'Impassioned at debate I remember . . . I listened then, I'll listen now.'

'This is not a college debate, and I didn't know you lived here . . . unfortunate.'

'You're Provisional I.R.A.?'

'Obviously.'

Millicent put the two bottles on the scrubbed deal table and dropped her voice: 'Those two horrors inside . . . with faces like that . . . I can see them doing anything . . . not you.'

'One has three A levels and I find their faces less horrific than the painted ones round your walls.'

'You'll kill me, my parents, friends, a churchman, in cold blood?'

Lynam did not answer.

'You can maim, cripple, blind the innocent . . . for what?'

'You've never been colonised, you wouldn't understand.'

'I can try, if you can explain.'

The unafraid manner and arrogant voice seemed patronising. She had long flaxen hair, immaculate skin, and brown searching eyes, eloquent as her mother's but less vulnerable. Lynam felt suddenly docked by a hostile witness, a self-possessed, model girl with a modelled upper-class mind. Looking straight back she said:

'I don't have to.'

'You can't . . . you've had your student pub-crawls, your bedsit affairs, hitched about and got stoned, so now you're a graduate . . . work's a bore, what next . . . back-room politics with mindless killers . . . a taste of terror before you die . . . it's beyond contempt.'

Lynam did not react and said after quite a pause: 'You married?'

Surprised, Millicent glanced at her wedding ring: 'I was to have our first child in January . . . does that mean anything to you.'

'Capricorn.'

'What!?'

'Capricorn.'

'I don't think you're quite human.'

'Yesterday, Victoria Regina Magnifica gave five pounds for Irish famine relief and the same week five pounds to a British dog fund.'

'Yesterday?'

'She's still alive . . . when you stop killing us we'll stop killing you . . . it's as simple as that.'

'What have I . . . we . . . got to do with killing you?'

'Everything.'

'You're not sane.'

'Very, and human, and distressed about your child . . . if there's anything I can do?'

The door came in and Gallagher was suddenly standing in the pantry. He paused, looking from one girl to the other, walked between them picking up a cut-glass tumbler from the table on his way to the sink. Millicent left. Gallagher tapped off three full glasses and drank them without pause and then held the tumbler up to the light.

'Eighteenth-century Waterford; Huguenot rubbish.'

He dropped the tumbler: it shattered in the teak sink.

'A Protestant cultural victory . . . nicked the Book of Kells too . . . how goes it girl?'

'Fine.'

He looked at her for a moment in silence and then said: 'I like you Lynam.'

'You don't and it's reciprocal.'

Blinking oddly Gallagher ran his tongue round his upper lip and asked: 'Why?'

'Boasting your kills; sickening.'

'That a fact?'

Gallagher looked at her, his eyes moving slowly from her legs up her body to her face. 'Contrary bitch . . . you preach killing and puke on killers . . . two-faced . . . you're like your old man Lynam, a Republican fraud.'

He moved towards the door, turned as he opened it and said: 'One thing, Mise Eire nua,* a dodgy move . . . ' he flicked his pistol, 'and I'll be watching . . . I don't trust you.'

When Gallagher had left Lynam said quietly: 'Nor I, myself.'

Passing the table as Caldwell poured whiskey, Gallagher said: 'Enjoy it, Sir.'

'I'll try,' Caldwell said.

Leonard had pulled an ornate chair into the shuttered bay window, a solitary audience, aware of murmurs and movement round the table, the faces imprinted on his mind by the initial exchange. As time passed he would get to know each face in more detail, and cold action if it had to come would be that much more awful. He was aware of tension in himself as he listened to the McAleers' hammering above, and imagined the guttural roar of pigs and Saracens which would arrive from Lisnaskea within fifteen minutes or less.

Now as he saw Gallagher come padding down the room he realised that he was glad to see him. He had argued strongly with Burke against taking him on this job pointing out that he was epileptic, and might prove unpredictable. 'You'll be glad of him,' Burke had said. Gallagher approached, leaned towards Leonard and said quietly:

'Heard Lynam say to the daughter "if there's anythin' I can do".'

'They were at college together.'

Gallagher stood alongside Leonard watching the table: 'Smug . . . look at them . . . we should smash something . . . make them dance on the table, face the wall with their arms out.'

*The modern Kathleen ni Houlihan

'Pointless Jack, relax.'

'I will.'

Without warning Gallagher moved from the bay window towards bookshelves on either side of the fireplace that went from floor to ceiling. He stood there for a minute or so reading titles. He then put his pistol on the high mantelpiece, took out a book and read aloud: '*The Un-finished War*, by Eric Moore Ritchie.'

He opened the book and read from the fly leaf: 'The drama of Anglo-German Conflict in Africa in relation to the future of the British Empire . . . eight maps, published London, 1940 . . . includes campaigns in East Africa, Cameroons and Togoland.'

Gallagher paused and said: 'Or: who owns the Nig Nogs, their nuts and their nickel.'

He put back Eric Moore Ritchie took down another book and again read aloud: '*Pig Sticking or Hog Hunting*, by Sir Robert Baden-Powell. A complete account for sportsmen and others, published London, 1824.'

Gallagher looked at the Colonel and asked: 'Enoch's great-grand-daddy?'

He replaced Baden-Powell and said: 'Nothing in our culture to match that . . . makes you feel inferior . . . humble . . . we've a long way to go . . . we bog, we pig-in-the-parlour Irish . . . yes, Sir, a long way to go.'

He picked up a nearby chair, moved towards the table and sat, placing the chair between the Colonel and Boyd-Crawford.

'Would you like to pour me a dram, Sir?'

'Of course,' the Colonel said evenly.

The Colonel poured a generous measure.

'You buy Irish?'

'Northern Irish,' Canon Plumm said.

'We know; they boast no natives near the mash, we

have a long list of all such firms . . . I'll not discriminate . . . your good health.'

Gallagher drank and said: 'You're American Sir?'

'That is correct.'

'Caldwell . . . Fermanagh stock . . . good planter name . . . Nixon too . . . great people . . . must make you feel proud . . . kinship with high office . . . doing a book on the troubles, Professor?'

'Research.'

'Into what?'

'Ulster under Elizabeth the First.'

'The Virgin Queen in Ulster?'

'She didn't come here.'

'That a fact. No virgin either, was she? . . . But she could pick good butchers . . . men with big swords . . . big cannon balls . . . still does . . . nice day for killing . . . that's what the Paras said in Derry . . . Lizzie II's high-jumping men . . . kill in Irish means Church . . . cuill a wood . . . darkness and death . . . might teach you some Irish tonight . . . a few sad songs . . . we've got hundreds . . . but this war is not merry . . . it's ugly, very very ugly, and we'll keep it ugly till it's over.'

Gallagher drained the rest of his whiskey and looked in silence from face to face.

'I like talking, but you don't like what I say . . . it's the silence: I can tell . . . but as the night goes on the atmosphere may improve . . . we must hope for progress towards a general understanding of the underlying tensions that gulf our ancient cultures over seven centuries . . . we've been under . . . while you were lying.'

Gallagher suddenly hacked a cross on the patina of the hunting table with the bead of his pistol. 'The cross and the sword: the glory of Europe.'

He then placed it sideways on the table and spun it with his forefinger. As it twirled he said to Caldwell: 'This is what they do in your Westerns.'

It stopped with the nozzle facing Alex Boyd-Crawford: 'A fossil first!'

Gallagher took the hearing-aid clipped to Alex's handkerchief pocket and using it like a microphone asked loudly: 'Do you think there's any hope for peace in our time Sir?'

Alex jerked, pulling out the earpiece as Gallagher's voice exploded in his left eardrum. With a sudden movement Gallagher whipped the hearing-aid from his jacket and smashed it on the hearth.

'Deaf anyway . . . all of you . . . you'll hear and listen before we quit.'

Harriet broke the silence that followed: 'I think he means it Nobby.'

'Every word,' Gallagher said.

Impassive the Colonel turned to Leonard: 'Are you supposed to be in charge?'

Leonard did not reply and kept watching till he caught Gallagher's eye. Gallagher went to him and hunkered to listen.

'They'll be here soon.'

'I can't sit.'

'Then move around.'

The door leading to the front hall opened. Pacelli McAleer's black head appeared. He grinned and came in, followed immediately by Pascal carrying a canvas bag. Pascal smiled at Leonard.

'That's it, all nailed, wired and locked.'

Pacelli looked about the magnificent room with mock awe.

'Damn it, this is a powerful place.'

'It's a palace, man, a palace.'

'There's beds above big as a council kitchen.'

'Sleep a whole fambley.'

Both stared at a full length portrait of a judge in wig and red gown, a parchment in his hand.

'Like a house'd nourish ghosts,' Pascal said.

Pacelli grinned. 'Every class but the Holy Ghost.'

As Lynam came in from the pantry Pascal groped in the canvas bag and began issuing tear-gas masks. As Gallagher slipped one over his head, leaving it hang, he said:

'Christmas in August; thank you Santy; you're full of surprises.'

Leonard pointed towards the pantry door and said: 'Out there boys: three doors. Check them.'

The McAleers left followed by Gallagher. As Lynam moved to join Leonard she saw the hearing-aid smashed on the hearth.

'What provoked that?'

'Jack, tense like us . . . and a bit hung over.'

'The daughter's pregnant.'

Leonard did not react.

'Can we let her go?'

Leonard nodded.

'Now?'

'Not yet . . . How do you feel?'

'Scarified. What now?'

Leonard looked at his watch and said: 'Forces from demi-paradise.'

'How long?'

'They're late.'

As he spoke they heard in the distance the heavy-engined growling of Saracens, jeeps, and pigs in convoy a mile off or less. Leonard stood and went to the deep recess of the doorway giving to the long hall. Lynam followed and stood beside him, her heart jumping as the growl increased to a deep-throated roar. Gallagher was back in the room sitting in the chair Leonard had left, his pistol levelled at the table.

'The Army of the Empire full of beans and bitters, I could smell them coming.'

It was five minutes before the armoured wagons rolled up the long avenue to the wide front, scattering gravel, screeching to a standstill. Silence, then the sound of massive, steel-plated doors clanging shut, voices, cryptic orders, a search-light beaming through the glass panels of the tall front door. Lynam was shaking so badly she felt her legs would give. She whispered to Leonard:

'Martin.'

'Yes.'

It was the first time she had used his name.

'I can't.'

'Can't what?'

She was in deep shadow beside him.

'Kill.'

'Can you do the other?'

'I think so.'

Leonard nodded and said: 'On you go.'

She moved from the terror of keeping still into the beam of the Army search-light. She unlocked and unbolted the front door and went out. As she walked down the wide granite steps she was aware of shadows behind the Saracens and jeeps, the search-light tilted slightly to follow her descent. Pausing at a flagged break in the stairway and shading her eyes against the militant light she flung her voice towards the dark massive shapes.

'I want to speak to the Commanding Officer.'

'Over here,' a Sandhurst voice from the right said.

'Here,' she said, replying to the voice.

There seemed a thirty-second delay before she heard

the crunching of footsteps coming towards her over gravel, then the briskness of leather boots on stone. Then he was standing before her blocking the light, khaki, chain-mail pullover, wide leather belt, black beret. Looking straight at his chest she said:

'You know who we are?'

'I can guess.'

'Who we're holding?'

'The staff 'phoned details.'

'We want Daniel Quinn, Peter McIntyre and John Fannin brought here before tomorrow noon ... also a helicopter.'

He took out a notebook and began to write. She was tempted to say, can you not remember three names. She stayed silent. As he wrote the names he said: 'Top-ranking chaps?'

'Trained killers like you.'

Though his face was in shadow she could see his mouth stiffen.

'If not?'

'Can't you guess?'

'You'll have to say it.'

'We execute one at noon, then one every six hours.'

The officer repeated the names correctly, Lynam nodded and said: 'Any shock approach and it's over.'

Without warning he moved from light to darkness. As she turned to go up towards the front door the search-light went off. Now, she thought, expecting a dozen soldiers to stampede past her through the door like a pack of rugby forwards. Nothing happened. She reached the door, went in, closed, locked and rebolted it and heard Leonard's voice.

'Well?'

'He wrote down the names.'

'Rommel himself, what else?'

'Nothing, he listened and vanished.'

'What did it feel like?'

'Being on stage.'

'You did well.'

Lynam felt braced, exhilarated by action and wondered how it was that she was less afraid to face guns than fire them.

'What now?'

'Watch and wait.'

'Before I went out I meant what I said.'

'Won't come to that.'

They went into the living-room.

Alex Boyd-Crawford had moved from the table. Standing separately he seemed shocked, lost. Harriet went to him: He watched her mouth, lipreading.

'Dear Alex . . . come on, sit down.'

'I'm all right.'

'Are you frightened?'

'Perhaps they thought I looked dangerous . . . do you think I look dangerous?'

'You look very much the bookish, kindly, broken-down landlord.'

Alex looked into those eyes he knew so well. 'You were pointedly rude at dinner.'

'What did I say?'

'You know well what you said.'

She shrugged and muttered, 'All true.'

He attempted a smile. 'Real truth, my dear, leads to crucifixions.'

Harriet did not hear. She was looking from Gallagher to Leonard:

'What do they intend?'

'Red chap wants to shoot us all, that's very clear.'

Without looking at him she said:

'If anything happens you, Alex – me – any – or all

of us, I want you to know how very, very dear you are to me.'

'And the word you avoid?'

'You are very, very dear to me.'

Gallagher now moved towards Alex Boyd-Crawford and flicked his pistol at him indicating the pantry door. Alex got up and shuffled out. Pacelli followed, taking the canvas bag into the pantry. As the door closed Harriet said to Millicent:

'I know it's happening, but I can't quite believe it.'

It was Caldwell who replied.

'People near death experience similar feelings.'

Harriet knew that he had said something apt, but the sound of his voice was so repugnant that she rejected the meaning. She watched for a response in her husband's face. There was none. Caldwell went on talking.

'As a child I remember being told how Christ had been crucified ... an Irish servant girl ... she told it well. I was stunned and said "They were bad men ... they should all be killed for doing that ... " '

She glanced at Caldwell and saw him nod towards Leonard and Lynam:

'That's how they feel, about you people ... they've never grown up ... dangerous deadly children.'

Without quite knowing what she meant Harriet said:

'Out of the mouths of babes.'

In the pantry Alex stood watching, frightened. Gallagher motioned him to sit. Pacelli groped deep in the bag, took out a small chemist's bottle and shook ten tablets onto the table. Gallagher brought a glass of water and indicated that Alex was to take the tablets. When he hesitated, Gallagher swung the pistol across his chest above his shoulder to inflict Alex, knowing that he would put both hands up protectively, an old monkey, defenceless before elemental violence. Gallagher dropped his arm as Alex picked up the tablets and swallowed them with water.

'Open your mouth.'

Alex could not hear. Gallagher opened his own mouth to demonstrate. Alex complied. Gallagher peered in, nodded, and said loudly in Alex's ear: 'Keep it shut inside . . . your mouth . . . understand?'

Alex nodded.

They went back to the living-room. Gallagher pointed at one of the two deep, wing-backed chairs at the fireside. Alex sat in one chair, grey, blinking at his smashed hearing-aid on the tiled hearth. The faces round the table watched, deeply concerned, questioning. After the initial exchange of looks Alex kept his head averted. Harriet moved from the table to the chair opposite. When he looked up she was asking with her eyes if he was all right. He made a small gesture with his hands, which said: 'It's nothing, I'm all right.' She nodded, relieved.

Gallagher winked at Leonard as he moved to the deep recess of the doorway that led to the hall. He sat in shadow watching the front door. The light from the bay window showed up the unreal pallor of his profile. Statuesque he hugged his knees, rigid, like a dog who has scented quarry and waits for it to break.

Leonard had picked up a chair and was now sitting alongside Lynam. An hour passed in total silence. The fire went low. Pascal added a few logs to the fire-basket and examined the Tomkin clock on the mantel and went back to sit beside Pacelli on the magnificent couch in buttoned grey velvet. Side by side they maintained the same fixed half-smile as though permanently in front of a camera.

Alex had fallen asleep in fifteen minutes and, fifteen minutes later, Harriet. Millicent leafed unreading through a copy of *Homes and Gardens*. The Colonel and Caldwell were well through a bottle of Bushmills. Now and then they spoke in low voices. A helicopter passed low over the house, landed somewhere on the left. When the twirling blades stopped Lynam looked at Leonard who muttered:

'Couldn't be.'

Another hour passed before Lynam said:

'This is deadly.'

'What?'

'Everything. I feel sick.'

'Nausea?'

'Not that sort.'

'Want to read?'

'Couldn't.'

'Drink?'

'Yes.'

'Not wise.'

'What is?'

'You should eat first.'

'I know.'

'Can you try?'

She shook her head. Leonard went to the table and picked up a tumbler. The Colonel poured a three-finger measure. Leonard nodded thanks, topped up with water and came back with the glass to Lynam. Without looking from the doorway Gallagher said:

'Slainte.'

'Slainte leat,' Lynam said.

'Want some?' Leonard asked Gallagher.

Gallagher shook his head.

'That's all you're getting,' Leonard said to Lynam. 'You must try to eat.'

She nodded. He indicated Gallagher: 'He needs it more than you and he's doing without.'

'I don't need bloody lectures.'

Five minutes later she said: 'Sorry . . . I feel odd.'

'Not my idea of a night out either.'

'The last.'

'It's going to work, I can feel it.'

'How?'

'Instinct.'

From the chair Alex Boyd-Crawford muttered indistinctly:

'October . . . no growth . . . must finish picking apples before the frost comes . . . they still bear . . . old and cankered but still bear. My leaky cider press . . . no matter . . . nothing matters . . . who's right? The Secretary . . . the tribal chain gangs . . . fraudulent . . . or maybe me . . . don't know . . . know nothing.'

When he began to snore Harriet went to him and did something to make him stop.

For half an hour Lynam sipped the whiskey. The ticking of the Tomkin clock became more insistent. The room seemed to lengthen slowly. Then she became aware of gradual grotesque distortion as the living flesh of each face turned grey in a fixed grimace of death. For a minute she thought she would scream as her caged heart leaped in beating terror. Normality returned.

'Can't we do something?' she asked.

Leonard thought for a moment, then winked over at Pascal and made a blowing mime with his mouth into both hands. When Pascal looked doubtful Leonard winked encouragement. Pascal took a tin whistle out of the canvas bag. When he began to play the expression on the faces of both brothers changed to one of rapt involvement, as the single note clarity carried not only its own beauty but a racial memory, evocative as the fields, battles and defeats – the music celebrated or lamented. Watching the lack of effect the music had on those round the table and aware of its impact on herself Lynam understood again why the first Elizabeth had hung Irish pipers as felons. The colour of melody neutralised the creeping terror of this ending day and the day that had to come.

The seeming naïvety of Hugh and Rosie McAleer's two sons masked, she thought, deeper roots, a culture old as pastoral Europe, clamped by history to the dead autocracy of Rome and the arrogant mess of the British Raj, themselves swamped now by the tinfoil gleam of Americana and the creeping threat of Russian paralysis, all beliefs and systems blending as old cultures died, inevitable and melancholy as the music, as the drying of tributaries with the deepening of great rivers.

At the table the talk continued in low voices, Canon Plumm turning up cards, Millicent now asleep on her arms.

'Haunting,' Caldwell said.

'Noise,' the Colonel said.

'Very special.'

'Repetitive I thought.'

'Do you know the language?' the Canon asked.

'No but . . .'

'You'd like to?'

'It's the key.'

'To what?' Canon Plumm muttered. 'Bingo? Chicken in the rough, non-stop reels of jig-jig trash? The great, great show with endless whining lamentations manufactured by jackeens for plough-boys and shopgirls . . . what they want . . . what they get . . . what they deserve . . . Irish culture! My idea of hell.'

Caldwell smiled: 'God is not a proven Protestant, Canon!'

'Damnation for me,' the Canon said, 'if he's Roman Catholic.'

'You grow a little acid, John,' the Colonel said.

'Accurate and angry,' the Canon said. 'Hatred, they're good at that, and killing . . . they breed good killers, poor leaders.'

Almost inaudibly Caldwell muttered, 'Next to love the sweetest thing is hate.'

The transistorised voice of a BBC news-reader came from the doorway. They paused, listening alert. It was too faint to hear.

'All so unfair,' the Colonel said. 'We were never absentees, my grandfather cut rents to half and nil during the famine, mortgaged the estate to feed tenants, Catholic and Protestant, one of my cousins signed the Treaty for the Irish side, Harriet's father was related through marriage to Lloyd George . . . lunacy.'

He paused looking into his whiskey. 'I knew Erskine well . . . a good actor . . . in his heart of hearts he didn't believe in nationalism any more than I do.'

'Did he say so?' Caldwell asked.

'I could sense it . . . it's a disease.'

'Sadly,' Caldwell said, 'most nations suffer from it.'

'The cancer is in this room and may kill us shortly.'

After a minute Caldwell asked: 'Could we, should we try something?'

'If you want to die *now* Stuart, yes, but I think they'll let you go.'

'It didn't sound . . . '

''Course they will . . . doesn't do to shoot Americans . . . ancient order . . . strong subscribers.'

'No special preference for humble churchmen I expect?' Canon Plumm asked.

'I doubt it John.'

Gallagher's voice came from the doorway, bleak as a Derry street in January: 'Pity you're not a bishop, Sir.'

In a very low voice the Colonel asked: 'Could he have heard?'

'Apparently,' Caldwell said.

'Unnatural.'

'Every way,' the Canon added.

Caldwell was about to say something when the volume of Gallagher's transistor was turned to a news-reader's voice in mid-sentence.

' . . . at the Armstrong Estate in County Fermanagh the Army are standing by. The kidnappers are demand-ing the release of three leading Provisionals from the Maze camp at Belfast. They want them brought to Inver Hall by helicopter. If this demand is not met, they say they will kill the first hostage at noon tomorrow and thereafter one every six hours. Colonel Armstrong served under General Montgomery in the African cam-paign and was awarded the D.S.O. Also hostage is Alex-ander Boyd-Crawford, member of the old Stormont Parliament for over twenty years. An American pro-fessor and a Protestant clergyman are among the six being held.'

Gallagher switched off as the news-reader switched to the next topic. All awake and listening in silence except Alex. Harriet was the first to speak. To Millicent she said:

'We don't exist dear.'

'I noticed,' Millicent said.

'I published two poems in a school magazine over forty years ago, but I expect that's hardly newsworthy . . . but you dear are a Bachelor of Arts.'

She paused looking from face to face: 'Bachelor? . . . Should it not be a Spinster of Arts . . . sounds miserable . . . dog's nice . . . who likes bitch . . .

bulls are magnificent ... cows stupid ... boars fierce ... sows eat their young ... the language itself is perverse to the female ... men only ... we're under sentence and the BBC don't know we exist.'

Harriet's voice was a great deal less slurred than earlier, but she looked haggard ... Suddenly she asked Leonard: 'What have you done to Alex?'

Leonard did not reply.

'He's a light sleeper ... drugged him?'

Again no reply.

Harriet went to the table and held a tumbler towards the whiskey bottle. The Canon poured a measure. She held the glass under the nose of the bottle till he splashed in another finger. Millicent was again trying to sleep with her head on the table. Harriet went round and whispered to her. Millicent got up and went to the wing-backed chair. Before sitting Harriet stood looking at the McAleers with detached curiosity much as people at a zoo examine creatures they have never seen before. The McAleers looked at each other, smiled, looked back at Harriet who continued to stare, till Pascal asked:

'Can you see horns Ma'am?'

'Pardon?' Harriet asked.

Pacelli said: 'My feet are cleft, but we kicked football with the best!'

'Monaghan Minors '71.'

Harriet understood nothing of what they said and muttered vaguely, 'Yes', shook her head, sat down and turned to Canon Plumm.

'Was I rude tonight at dinner John?'

The Canon mumbled: 'No consequence.'

'I'm sorry.'

'Nothing ... nothing at all.'

Both the Colonel and Caldwell were aware that another apology was due. It was not forthcoming.

Silence again and through it Lynam saw Millicent looking steadily into her eyes. She returned the look without hostility until Millicent turned her head and closed her eyes.

'Can't you let her go?'

'Who?'

'The daughter.'

'Not yet.'

Leonard took the empty glass from her hand, put it on the floor and said: 'Your hands are ice cold.'

'I know.'

Quarter of an hour passed. Without looking at him Lynam said: 'I want to make love.'

Leonard did not reply till she asked: 'Can we?'

'You're joking.'

'Don't you want?'

It seemed to Leonard that the pitch of her voice had increased. He said: 'Talk low.'

'What?'

'Impossible.'

She nodded towards the pantry and said: 'In there.'

There was a minute's silence before Leonard replied.

'Madness.'

'I can't hear you.'

'Insane.'

'Sane . . . we're dead.'

'Far from it . . . very far.'

'Are you afraid?'

Leonard leaned very close to her and said: 'Your voice.'

'What about it?'

'It's carrying.'

'Who cares?'

With a movement of his eyes Leonard indicated Gallagher.

'You might tomorrow.'

'There's no tomorrow.'

Leonard shrugged. The whiskey and seven hours of extreme tension had begun to tell.

'Try to sleep,' he said.

She lay back in the chair and closed her eyes without answering. He was right. An absurd provocative notion which she would have welched on had he agreed. Why? To tempt him, humiliate herself, goad Gallagher, shock the atavistic McAleers, confirm the listening table in the poor opinion already held, or the reflex of a sad song and the bitter knowledge of betrayal, the total certainty that this was the last night of her life. Pointless trying to disentangle. Then she was in the pantry with Leonard, the door locked and she could hear Gallagher outside whispering to the McAleers:

'The Hound of Ulster is screwing the bitch from the Pale . . . grave dereliction of duty boys . . . they should be shot both of them; I'll see to it when the job's over!' Then she saw Gallagher go up to Alex Boyd-Crawford and shoot him twice through the head. Terrified she unlocked the pantry door that led to the hall, ran down the wide flags, opened the front door and out. It was grey daylight. As she ran down the granite steps she heard glass shatter. A single shot pierced a burning pain in her womb. She fell. As she tried to get up she was kneeling facing the bay window looking into Gallagher's cold face. He was pointing his pistol directly at her. She screamed.

Leonard had such a tight grip on her wrist that it hurt. She was trembling. Everyone in the room was looking at her except Alex Boyd-Crawford who was deep asleep. Leonard said:

'It's all right.'

She saw the clock on the mantel – 1.55 – and realised she had been asleep for almost an hour.

'Did I . . . ?'

The faces at the table looked away, answering her unasked question. Harriet stood and moved towards the pantry door. Leonard said:

'Go with her . . . and when you come back, eat, or take a pill and sleep.'

She could sense real irritation in his voice. She got up and followed the Colonel's wife into the pantry. As the door closed Leonard motioned Pascal to stand alongside the door. The Colonel's wife had gone into the cloak-room toilet off the pantry. As she waited Lynam could hear, or imagined she could hear, retching. On the pan-elled wall someone had pinned recipes from newspapers and magazines. She tried to read one of them. The words had no meaning. She heard the toilet flush. The cloakroom door opened. Footsteps and the scrape of a chair and Harriet's voice saying:

'Do sit, please.'

Lynam hesitated, then complied. It was a request more than an order, and she felt weak. She sat at the other end of the table facing the older woman, avoiding her eyes.

'Look at me please.'

Lynam looked.

'Will you . . . they . . . shoot us all dead?'

'Depends.'

'They won't do what you ask.'

'They might.'

Harriet shook her head.

'Nobby's not important . . . old family but not important . . . you're off target dear . . . I know a dozen houses more suitable for this operation.'

There was a considerable silence before Harriet began again.

'Odd how floods, bombs, hurricanes, earthquakes happen elsewhere to others . . . never to oneself . . . I wasn't sick with fright in there, I don't care when I die provided it's quick . . . you know Milly?'

'We shared French tutorials.'

'She's pregnant.'

'I know.'

'Told you?'

'Yes.'

'Will she be sacrificed to Republican gods?'

'No.'

'That's something . . . I suppose.'

Harriet studied the pitted quarry tiles on the floor for thirty seconds. Her face had the stillness and depth of an El Greco portrait, hurt, haunted staring eyes which a faint sudden smile now altered to subtle knowingness as she looked up to speak.

'French?'

'Sorry?'

'You did French?'

'Yes.'

'What else?'

'Irish.'

'You know David Greene?'

'Yes.'

'Wonderful beard.'

'He's a good scholar.'

'Do you like Dylan Thomas?'

'Not as much as Kavanagh.'

'Really?'

Lynam tapped the table then nodded towards the dresser and said: 'I prefer this to that.'

Harriet did not understand.

'Which to what?'

'Scrubbed deal to a Welsh dresser.'

She smiled for the first time and said: 'Yes, Milly read English and French . . . but no real empathy . . . *Henry the Fifth* troubles me . . . do you like it?'

'No.'

'Nor do I . . . inexcusable of Shakespeare, bad as the Old Testament . . . reeks of blood and empire . . . Nobby loves it . . . you're like a cousin of mine, Dolly Travers, incredibly like . . . dead poor Dolly, happy life . . . never married. Thought she wasn't happy but a hundred times more so than . . . I feel quite exhilarated at the idea of sudden extinction . . . Mother was accomplished . . . the piano . . . played with Paderewski in a drawing room once . . . I was a child of eight . . . And Paderewski said after it was the most beautiful rendering of a Chopin Prelude he had ever heard. Poor mother was radiant. Everyone clapped. Father was Welsh . . . shrewd at business. His money kept this place going . . . his money . . . my money . . . '

Harriet paused and studied Lynam for a moment.

'We're sister Celts, you and I . . . I can sing a little . . . though not much to sing about these days . . . Would you like to get me a glass of water . . . please.'

Lynam brought the glass of water.

'After Derry I wept, you know, and Nobby was overwhelmed . . . true . . . he's human . . . all of us . . . very human . . . so terribly sad what we do to each other don't you think? He tried to 'phone Frank Carrington . . . couldn't get through . . . retired Colonels in Fermanagh don't count for much . . . rather silly really holding us . . . he's liked . . . always Catholics on the staff . . . and what you're doing won't be popular with Catholics or Protestants . . . of that I'm sure . . . but you're here and that's it . . . war is a series of unfortunate blunders . . . like marriage.'

She inhaled deeply on a cigarette, exhaling through her mouth and nose. She then finished the glass of water.

'That red-headed youth, such astonishing energy . . . such hatred, are you like that?'

'No.'

'Do you love?'

Again Harriet asked Lynam: 'Do you?'

'Do you?'

Harriet studied the floor as though she had forgotten Lynam's presence. When she began it was as though she was talking to herself.

'Once upon a time a warrior went to war. When he came back he woke half dreaming in a grey dawn distressed and crying for a comrade who had died.'

She paused for ten seconds, looked up and said: 'You can fight the living my dear, not the dead . . . marriage is such a cruel trap for some that they long for . . . '

She searched about her memory and found:

> 'That high capital where Kingly death
> Keeps his pale Court in beauty and decay.

Shelley, poor boy . . . why did I tell you that?'

'We're both dead.'

'Yes . . . Nobby says I'm maudlin . . . would you like some coffee? . . . I would.'

'Where?'

Harriet pointed.

'In that cupboard, instant, the kettle's there . . . power point beside the sink, we keep it here . . . there's a mile of corridor to the kitchen proper . . . What happened to Maggie Reilly and the Johnstons?'

'Pardon?'

'The staff?'

'They were locked out.'

'Ah! . . . Were they frighened I wonder?'

'I hope not.'

'You're a feeling girl . . . I could sense that . . . Milly's cold . . . my own flesh and blood . . . sad.'

Lynam moved about making the coffee.

'Your mother alive?'

'Yes.'

'Father?'

'Yes.'

'Family?'

'Two brothers.'

'Like you?'

'Apolitical.'

There was a kind of silence until Harriet broke it by asking: 'What killed you?'

'Rejection.'

'Always the same story . . . one thing puzzles me, I can understand those who want to kill themselves, not those who kill others . . . you look all wrong for the part . . . Nobby's professional . . . he looks right don't you think? . . . Hatred is so sad . . . personal hatred I know only too well, but to hate an entire people, race, sect or class, is so blind, so stupid, so unending, so universal, it makes one despair . . . When that red youth smashed Alex's hearing-aid I knew then it was serious.'

The electric kettle began to boil. Lynam moved to switch it off.

'Will they kill Caldwell the American?'

'I doubt it.'

'Politically embarrassing.'

Lynam nodded.

'They're embarrassing anyway, most of them . . . he's a world authority you know . . . medieval military manoeuvres or something incredible . . . prestigious fellowship, a year's sabbatical, New England University . . . Divorce . . . said his wife was beautiful, but lacked a mind . . . I think he thinks I have no mind . . . could be right, I behave oddly at times . . . Nobby thinks he's a genius . . . met at the British Embassy in New York last year, some military memorial thing. John Freeman introduced them . . . I think he's illiterate – not Freeman, Caldwell.'

Harriet stubbed her cigarette on an ashtray and asked: 'Do you think he's queer?'

Lynam could not answer. Harriet went on: 'You can't tell nowadays . . . nothing's certain. Has God lost interest do you think?'

'I don't believe in God.'

'Nor do I . . . Are the two dark ones brothers?'

'Yes.'

'Don't look quite the full shilling do they? You've put down eleven cups, that's nice.'

'Yes.'

'Good idea. You don't say much . . . perhaps you dislike me?'

'No.'

'I embarrass you?'

'No.'

'What do you feel?'

Lynam looked into the liquid lostness of those brown unhappy eyes in that blurred finely-modelled face. In ten minutes she seemed to understand the oblique confusion and compassion of this strange woman's mind better than she had ever understood her own mother.

'I must know.'

'Pity,' Lynam said. 'For all of us.'

Harriet continued to stare and and the subtlety Lynam was aware of earlier returned.

'But you're here to kill if need be.'

Lynam shook her head.

'Were you forced to come?'

'I can't explain . . . sorry.'

'Your hands are trembling.'

'Yes.'

'Are you afraid?'

'Yes.'

'I fear death too . . . did you believe me when I said I didn't?'

'Not quite.'

The door opened. Pascal stood smiling. Harriet stood and left the pantry.

There was silence in the long room as Lynam placed the tray of coffee on the table. Harriet took a cup and passed the others round. Lynam supplied Pascal, Pacelli, Leonard and Gallagher. As she sat beside Leonard he said:

'You were a while out there.'

'Yes.'

'Talking?'

'Listening.'

'Can you eat?'

As she looked at the food without interest, Pascal came over, took a silver serving spoon and put some potato and cauliflower salad on a plate. He pointed at the cold pork, tongue, and underdone beef.

'No meat, Pascal . . . thanks.'

'Sure?'

'Certain.'

As Pascal spooned mayonnaise she glanced round at Leonard. He was staring straight ahead avoiding her eyes. Deliberately? She moved to join the brothers, Pacelli shifting on the couch, tucking his legs under tailorwise. As she ate they smiled encouragement. The food was distasteful and their concern overwhelming. It made her feel unworthy, fraudulent. As the feeling increased she stopped eating. The plate began to tremble in her hand. Pascal took it from her and pulled up a chair to screen her from the table.

'Ate a lough more Bella. The grub'll steady you.'

As she began to pick at the food Pascal said: 'You were a while with the ould one.'

She nodded.

'Seems odd. Touched?'

'Strange,' Lynam said.

'You'd know that from her talk.'

In a very low voice Lynam asked: 'Did I scream over there?'

'A whimper . . . nothing.'

'You dropped off.'

'Before that?' she asked.

The brothers looked at each other pretending not to understand. Pascal shook his head: 'A dream I'd say.'

'Aye, you were asleep,' Pacelli explained.

She looked from one to the other gratefully and said: 'You lie beautifully . . . both of you . . . Are you boys afraid?'

'Scared stiff,' Pascal said. 'The stomach's in knots.'

'Constant fright,' Pacelli added. 'Natural.'

'You don't show it.'

'We don't let on . . . it's there.'

'Keep smilin' . . . stick together.'

Pacelli nodded towards the hunting table.

'You're fit to talk to those folk.'

'Martin too, if he wanted.'

'And Jack's afeered of nothin' in this world . . . go to hell for his friends.'

'He is hell,' she said.

As she looked over, Gallagher's left hand went up

slowly. He tapped his left ear, then pointed upwards with his forefinger, eyes dilated, a tense listening image.

The chalk-white face turned towards Leonard in the bay window. Leonard went and hunkered close.

'Hear!?'

'Nothing.'

A minute or more passed before Gallagher said: 'Rats on the back roof, four or more . . . hear!'

As Leonard shook his head a slate, scrape, or noise of slip came down distinctly through the house. Five seconds of utter silence followed. Leonard looked towards the McAleers and pointed at Alex Boyd-Craw-ford. The brothers moved as one carrying the inert body to the main hall. This took place so promptly that there was a pause before it registered that something serious had happened and was about to change everything. Leonard moved back to the bay window. Lynam sat up very straight knowing what might now occur. Muzzy from sleep Harriet stood.

'What are you . . . ?'

Half stumbling, almost sleep-walking, she moved towards the door.

'What are you doing with Alex?'

Gallagher blocked the doorway and gave a small flicking movement with his left hand in much the same way as parents dismiss small children who have broken their concentration. Harriet kept coming.

'I am not afraid, and will not sit by while . . . '

Gallagher's pistol whipped across her face so quickly that those in the room saw only the effect of the impact. Suddenly she was on her knees facing the fireplace, a welt from eye to cheek-bone, blood in her mouth. The Colonel was on his feet, veins swelling in his neck. Gallagher said, levelling at him:

'If you want.'

As he spoke two pistol shots sounded in the hall. Looks of electrified horror on all faces. Gallagher motioned the Colonel to sit by pointing with his free hand.

Still on her knees, Harriet seemed to be looking for something on the floor, a denture at the leg of the hunting table. Crying, Millicent recovered these for her mother. The Colonel and Canon Plumm helped her to the couch. From the hall the sound of the bolts being withdrawn, the door opening. The search-light was switched on, then switched off as the door was closed and rebolted. The McAleers came back into the room unsmiling.

Sick, ashamed, Lynam turned her back and stood looking at the design of the tapestry curtains in the high bay window. It was swimming before her eyes. Then Leonard's voice saying to the Colonel:

'You've got one minute from now to tell them outside and get back, and they've got three to get clear . . . one more sound after, anywhere in or near the house, and we execute the next.'

The Colonel went out. It was already breaking light. Under the bay window he saw Alex's prone body, a canvas bag tied over the head. The Colonel spoke with the Commanding Officer and returned at once. When he came in Millicent was placing a cushion under her mother's head. She had replaced the dentures and was holding a napkin over the gash in her mother's face.

Lynam went out to the hall. Gallagher saw her face as she passed and said: 'Necessary.'

She did not answer. She stood in the middle of the hall, the bulk of the armoured cars distinct through the front door. Near dawn. She could not display weakness in the room and would need time for composure to return.

'Don't stand there,' Gallagher said.

She moved to the cover of the door opposite. The thing was to exclude totally the reality of nightmare that seemed to grow with the breaking light. In the other doorway Leonard was whispering with Gallagher, both checking their wrist-watches, one looking up the dark stairwell, the other watching the door, both tense.

Coolfada . . . the smell of the sea, the astonishing greenness of grass that grew in lumps from the thatch, the peace of the sky and all the cats named after saints and townlands. People came to the house every evening because her grandmother had the cure for shingles. Once she was allowed to sit on the creepie and watch. The old woman placed twigs in the glowing turf, withdrew them glowing and went round a woman's stricken face half an inch from the skin saying prayers in Irish. One summer's day, a neighbour man came with a mongrel terrier. When he was inside the terrier chased and caught a white kitten and crushed it with a snap. She ran with it into her grandmother, screaming, warm blood on her hands. Her grandmother wrapped the kitten in brown paper, washed her hands and went out to the potato patch. As she buried it, she said:

'Some dogs kill cats, some men kill other men . . . the sea, hunger, disorder, old age, aye and a broken heart, night brings day brings night . . . death comes . . . don't cry love, it's life.'

The one image of Coolfada that she had wanted to forget had jerked back now with sickening vividness. The blood was on her hands now as it had been twenty years ago. If Coolfada conjured images of blood and death, there was no refuge in memory. Her eyes were closed. She did not see Leonard cross the hall. She heard him say:

'You'll have to come back . . . deadly out here.'

When she looked he thumbed at the wide stairwell leading up into the darkness of the house.

'Did he have to be so brutal?'

'She's all right . . . sitting up.'

Leonard waited. Lynam ran the back of her hand up both cheeks to ensure that they were dry and went back to the living room. Gallagher had moved the two chairs from the bay window and now swung back the heavy curtains. He unclasped the shutters. As he folded them back Pascal switched off the lights. A dim light filled the room. Millicent stood, her body shaking, as she said directly to Gallagher:

'Bastard, sickly cowardly murdering bastard.'

Suddenly she turned to Lynam.

'Are these your friends? A one-eyed dummy, two imbeciles and a sadist . . . ! My Christ, you're sick . . . ! All of you . . . sick!!'

The effect on Gallagher was almost physical. For ten seconds he could scarcely speak with fury. The first words coming in a whisper: 'Stuffed bitch . . . your mind's feeble as your tongue.'

Suddenly he shouted: 'Why are we sick. Come on, answer. Why?! Let's hear, any, all of you . . . come on . . . why?! Answer . . . you know it . . . you are it.'

In the silence that followed Leonard said quietly to the Colonel: 'Your wife was foolhardy Sir. Lucky she's alive.'

'That's arguable,' Harriet muttered.

'I would advise you,' Leonard said, 'to warn your daughter that she has no licence to insult . . . that, for the time being, is our privilege.'

The Colonel did not look at Leonard as he asked: 'Is this how you treat prisoners . . . wage war?'

Before Leonard could respond Gallagher cut in, his

176

face rigid with hatred: 'You talk of war and prisoners? You!'

He flicked his pistol.

'When we look for common rights the way you got your empire, all your lackeys in the Press and Commons yap; hang them, hang them, hang them. Mother of Parliaments? A fat knacker's wife who's flayed half the bloody world . . . and you think the world is with you? Such shits they say . . . such lying bullying hypocrites . . . with your mock monarchy and zoo-keeping dukes and public schools, all stiff upper prick and regiments of back-street rats and buggering Horatios, you have deported, degraded, starved and tortured us and still do . . . and no apology and never will . . . but smirk and snigger at stupid Paddy, dirty Paddy,

> Ugly superstitious Paddy,
> Paddy drop-out, Paddy drunk
> Paddy half-wit, Paddy Punk.'

Gallagher moved round the table as the words came savaging from his mouth. He paused at the end of the sideboard beneath an oil painting of a First World War Brigadier. Suddenly he elbowed a magnificent oriental soup tureen. It went sliding, spinning, down the long sideboard, scattering ornamental plates and silver before it shattered to the floor. With a back whip of his pistol he tore the face of the Brigadier.

'You smash us for seven hundred years, you haven't quit yet and you wonder why we hate you . . . hate is a nothing word for what we feel.'

The Colonel looked from Gallagher's livid face to the torn portrait and the smashed ware. A spitting mini-Hitler . . . pointless to argue with such hysterical hatred. As he thought this he heard himself say coldly:

'That was an Irishman leading other Irishmen.'

'To free small nations! . . . don't make me vomit.'

Gallagher returned to the doorway. Pascal and Leonard took up screened positions at the edge of the window. Pacelli sat at the far end of the room near the pantry door. Lynam sat in the corner alongside the Sheraton table near Leonard.

A quarter of an hour passed in silence. Nothing but the ticking of the clock and the Gothic screech of a peacock. Harriet stood. Sound of smaller birds, the first signs of light. She knew this from innumerable dawns. She walked to the bay window, saw Alex's prone body, then looked away to the lake beyond the half circle of military wagons. Grey, utterly still, mist hung, autumnal as though waiting and aware of the coming winter. There were a few faint stars very high, and faint tinctures of pink and red. She had seen a painting once in someone's house all grey and black and although she knew something awful had happened, and that something more awful was impending, she forced herself to say:

'Daybreak . . . Sunday . . . reminds me of a painting I saw in someone's house. We sleep when the world's most beautiful.'

'I wouldn't stand there,' Gallagher said.

'Will you smash me again if I do?'

'Dangerous,' Leonard said.

'Dangerous?'

Harriet looked with incredulity at the pistols and smiled: 'Quite a sense of humour . . . I like that.'

She turned from the window and looked towards the corner. Lynam was glad of the grey, half light. Harriet quoted: '*L'aurore grelottante en robe rose et verte*. How are you?'

'How are you?' Lynam asked, scarcely audible.

Harriet's voice wobbled as she said: 'Alive . . . but lacking a dear friend.'

She went back to the table and sat close to the wing-

178

backed chair occupied by Millicent who said: 'I wouldn't talk to them.'

Harriet stared at the dead ashes in the grate and spoke with unexpected edge: 'Alex was dragged out and shot dead while two military gentlemen sat by.'

'Mother, please.'

'Doing nothing . . . there are times when one must do something regardless of military hand-books and personal safety.'

Caldwell said, very quietly: 'You don't seem to . . . '

'I understand precisely what's going on, and what's likely to occur.'

In the silence that followed Millicent covered her face and kept it covered while she cried. Harriet put a hand on her daughter's head and looked over at Lynam. When the effect of the crying and Harriet's eyes became unbearable Lynam stood and whispered to Leonard:

'For Christ's sake Martin.'

Without looking at Lynam, or back at the table, Leonard said: 'She can go . . . and the American.'

From the doorway Gallagher frowned and shook his head. Leonard shrugged much as to say 'they're going anyway'. There was a silence before they adjusted to what had been said.

'Now?' the Colonel asked.

'Yes.'

Millicent stood. When she had kissed her father Harriet held her face for a moment, looking as though trying to read or recall something. Very gently, visibly moved, she kissed her daughter's forehead as a mother kisses the head of a very small child. In silence Caldwell shook hands in turn with the Colonel and Canon Plumm. Harriet had walked to the corner, her back to the table. Caldwell approached to make his farewell. She took his hand without turning to look at his face.

Gallagher stood to let them into the hall, followed them to the front door, opened it, relocking and rebolting when they were gone.

From where he stood Leonard could see them go down the granite staircase, across the half circle of gravel and out of sight behind the armoured wagons. Harriet came back to the table and lit a cigarette. The Colonel moved to the fireplace and stood looking at the Tomkin clock as though it contained some secret. The hands read 5.55. Canon Plumm, despite his fleshy face and bulky frame, seemed greyer, older, more exhausted than either the Colonel or his wife, as though he now fully realised that his calling would count for nothing in this ruthless double siege.

Gallagher went towards the pantry. Pascal moved to take his place in the doorway. Above the wood across the dark water the mist fell away leaving one bright star adrift in a metallic sky. Morning star. Lynam approached Leonard. Looking out and up she was aware of a numbness that swamped the nightmare hours and the coming fear. She wanted to pray but had forgotten how to begin or who to pray to . . . Lord have mercy, Christ have mercy.

'Remember Benediction?'

Leonard nodded and said:

'I used to sit and look at someone's back waiting for the priest to say "Morning star" . . . That I understood, nothing else.'

'Pagan at heart.'

Silence.

'It's quiet.'

'Very.'

'Did it affect you?'

'What?'

'The crying?'

'What do you think?'

'I think you must be very strong or very cold.'

Leonard shrugged slightly and indicated Pascal in the doorway.

'They're strong . . . they've got God on their side, the Mammy and Pearse's ghost.'

'Gallagher . . . he's terrifying.'

Leonard did not answer and she said: 'Psychopathic.'

'I can't judge . . . I'm here . . . so are you.'

'Why?'

Leonard shook his head as though the effort of answering such a complex question was impossible. A tired priest of violence, she thought, who had ceased to believe in the Creed. As he looked at her now she got a sense of something else; enigmatic, obscure, almost frightening.

'You are annoyed?'

'No.'

'By what I said.'

'No.'

'Last night, you're still angry?'

Again he shook his head. She remembered how he had said Gallagher would not waste words when it came to killing. Gallagher's racial and political bitterness were genuine. He was a natural mechanism of terror and disorder. He did not, never would, want peace and harmony. When it ended, and if the Leonards had control, they would despatch him. She realised now that Leonard's silence was more sinister, more frightening than Gallagher's savage outbursts. His surface warmth and ease masked an inner detachment, clinical, ice-cold. For the first time she felt utterly alone.

She looked back from the window. The Canon had his elbows on the table, eyes closed, supporting his head with his hands. The Colonel's wife was again in the wing-backed chair, the Colonel sitting alongside her. He was holding one of her hands in both of his. Lynam turned away, aware that she was intruding on something very personal. Harriet could sense emotion in her husband's voice as he said now:

'Always separate.'

She thought before replying.

'Very . . . I understand.'

'I did say at the time and since that if ever . . . ' He paused.

'You proved less than husband and lover?'

The Colonel nodded and said: 'You were free.'

'Free?'

'Yes.'

'I died that morning as a woman . . . you do understand that?'

Tears from the blood-hound eyes came down each side of his nose, disappearing in the grey, clipped moustache as he began to speak again unevenly.

'I was . . . am . . . abject . . . can say only . . . that despite . . . my very deepest truest love for you . . . ' He shook his head. 'No words.'

'Beyond words . . . I loved my illusion of you Nobby.'

'If we must die, can we die friends.'

'Well said.'

'You don't mock?'

Harriet shook her head.

'Friendship is better than love . . . much better.'

Again, as she had kissed her daughter, she now kissed her husband on the forehead, as humans kiss their beloved dead.

The pantry door opened. Gallagher came padding quietly down the long room. He had washed his face, damped and combed his hair and seemed, Lynam thought, alert, unafraid, almost celebratory. As he approached he said:

'Reading my face . . . what's written there Lynam? Thug? Criminal?'

The repulsion she had felt watching him come down the room must have been evident. Gallagher smiled and asked: 'Can we kiss?'

'Cut it Jack.'

'I am Ireland. She loves me, she should show it.'

Cunning logic to shame and establish her in brutal collusion before watching eyes from the table and wing-backed chair. Leonard had warned, and kept his back to her now as the warning stood roosting in smiling blackmail. She caught Pascal and then Pacelli's eye. If she refused and it caused Gallagher to explode it would throw Leonard and the brothers on a tight-rope. Leonard glanced at her and his expression read, 'It's nothing, do it and be done with it'. As she hesitated, Gallagher said, for her ears only:

'You wanted to screw with him four hours back.'

His voice normal he said again: 'A kiss . . . no more.'

As he neared she felt her stomach revulse. When their lips touched he caught her chin, inserting his tongue, his eyes open, staring. When it was over she felt defiled as though she had been kissed by a grinning corpse. She wanted to scream and claw with her nails at the mocking face. With a tremendous effort she controlled the churning in her stomach and kept her expression impassive. Emotionless, Leonard asked:

'Coffee? Can you make some?'

Lynam went straight to the pantry aware of Harriet's watching eyes as she walked. She stood trembling at the teak sink and rinsed her mouth out. 'Why am I trembling?' she thought. 'Death might be three hours away, less.' It was unlike her that self-control could be shattered by a sick Judas kiss, unreal that she should react soul and body with such revulsion. Intuitively she could sense an otherness in that kiss, something coming, hidden; what? Gallagher, none of them could tell what would happen before or at midday. Filling the kettle it seemed to her that the woman she had both liked and pitied last night now seemed enormously enviable. The victims had a dignity. She had joined with executioners, the army of the damned. As she thought this she knew the thought was treason. Waiting for the kettle to boil, Lynam took out the pistol and looked at it without the repulsion she had felt the evening before.

At the window Leonard asked: 'Did you have to do that?'

'She's soft, snivelling at the first whiff of action.'

'That didn't help.'

'I'm inhuman, a mindless killer, she said it, meant it . . . what's she? . . . a hysterical, gutless, middle-class yacker . . . and what's Burke at, sending her?'

'Good question.'

'She could wreck it.'

Leonard shook his head.

'I won't let her,' Gallagher said.

Leonard felt the impact of this jostle. He did not respond. Gallagher would never lead. He had the racial defect to a marked degree; too personal. It coloured his every word and act. Deliberateness was professional and although he had an ulcer from worry, slept badly and doubted much, Leonard knew that he was professional and said now:

'Leave her be, Jack, she'll learn.'

A BBC station-wagon came up the avenue, bounced onto the lawn and drove behind the half circle of Army wagons. Well in view, two men got up on the roof of the station-wagon, mounted a tripod camera and faced it towards the house.

'The eyes of the world,' Gallagher said.

Leonard nodded. Gallagher looked at his watch, it was 9.45.

'If the boys aren't here by twelve?'

'We go ahead.'

'We?'

Again Leonard knew what Gallagher was implying. Apart from five kills in action, he had executed, with cold efficiency, a Belfastman found guilty of treason. Now he presumed Leonard would ask him to execute the old man lying drugged under the bay window, half suggesting that he would use his position as leader to deputise the ugly work.

'I'll do that,' Leonard said.

'You will?'

Leonard nodded. Gallagher seemed surprised.

'Whatever you say Commandant.'

It was whatever he said and Gallagher would have to see unmistakably that he meant and did what he said. Three words prompted by an oblique question. He was now committed to action which he knew he could and would

do against the instinct which prompted avoidance.

Canon Plumm was alerted by the sound of the arriving station-wagon. He looked at the time and then went to the Colonel and said something. The Colonel nodded and pointed towards a row of book-shelves. The Canon read the titles for a while, then took down a book and leafed through it for five minutes. Lynam came in with coffee and passed it around. As they sipped coffee the Canon said:

'Sunday: I'd like to give a brief reading, do you mind?'

'Fine,' Leonard said.

The Canon sat at the head of the table, the Colonel one side, Harriet on the other. He put on spectacles, cleared his throat and read:

'A heavy yoke is upon the children of Adam, from the day of their coming out of their mother's womb, until the day of their burial into the mother of all. Fear not the sentence of death. Remember what things have been before and what follow after. This sentence is from the Lord on all flesh. The time of death matters not, nor the place, nor the manner. Therefore be ready, strive for high ideals. Be yourself. Do not feign affection, neither be cynical or without love for in the face of all disenchantment it is perennial as the grass. Nurture strength of spirit to shield you in sudden misfortune.'

The Canon paused before going on.

'In war and peace victims are many. Do not distress yourself with imaginings. Many fears are born of fatigue and loneliness. You are a child of the universe, no less than the trees and the stars; you have a right to be here, and whether or not it is clear to you the universe is unfolding as it should. Therefore be at peace with God whatever you conceive him to be. In the noise of life keep peace with your soul. With all its sham, drudgery, its conflicts and broken dreams . . . the world is still beautiful.'

In the stillness that followed the reading Gallagher said distinctly: 'Introibo ad altare Dei.'

Leonard responded almost inaudibly: 'Ad Deum, qui laetificat juventutem meam.'

Harriet had not come across this excerpt. Moved, she looked first at her husband, then at Canon Plumm and said:

'Very fitting . . . thank you Canon.'

The Canon closed the book of selected Sunday readings, considered for a moment, then stood and walked

186

towards Leonard and Gallagher. Without looking at either he said:

'I want you . . . all of you to understand that while I abhor your methods profoundly and dislike your politics, I hold no hatred in my heart.' He paused. 'I have often thought and said . . . things . . . unbecoming a man of God . . . we are what we are because of history.'

Gallagher scratched his chin with the muzzle of his pistol and said: 'History can be altered.'

Canon Plumm did not respond. He held out his hand towards Leonard. Leonard had to change his pistol from his right hand to his left hand in order to shake hands. Gallagher hesitated before following suit. As the Canon moved towards the McAleers and Lynam, Gallagher said quietly to Leonard:

'Plumm velvet, his ticket to heaven . . .'

Leonard did not reply. As the Canon sat after this the Colonel said: 'I would like to identify myself with what Canon Plumm just read and said.'

There was quite a silence before Leonard spoke.

'You understand, Sir, that we are at war.'

All waited for Leonard to elaborate. He did not. It was Gallagher who added without looking round: 'You know what war means: or should.'

Outside, Caldwell stood beside the British officer who was in radio contact. Twice he said: 'I understand.'

When he put down the military 'phone he shook his head. Caldwell looked away to the lake, looked at his watch and said: 'They'll let them be slaughtered?'

'They have masks . . . four pistols and three point blank targets . . . lunacy to go in.'

The August sun was now high over lake and forest flooding the long room with glorious light. Leonard stood at the edge of the window and watched Alex's prone figure, and the camera on the roof of the station-wagon. There was a light wind blowing across the water. The Tomkin clock ticked with unrelenting steadiness towards twelve. His heart slowed as he prepared for deliberate action. The three faces at the table were fixed in expressions of frozen fear and resignation. Gallagher was looking at Leonard intently. As the clock began to strike the McAleers stood. Lynam sat in the corner her face blank. Total silence as the last gong of the Tomkin clock faded. Leonard stepped back so that his shooting arm would not be visible. Holding his shooting wrist with his left hand he fired two shots towards the canvas covered head, pausing between each shot. After the first shot the body had twitched. It was now still. Gallagher nodded faintly. Lynam noticed a slight tremor in Leonard's hand as he inserted two fresh bullets, her mind empty as though some mechanism had excluded the brutality of fact. The McAleers blessed themselves. The faces at the table registered total incomprehension. It was the Colonel who asked:

'What? . . . Why did you fire?'

No one replied.

Lynam became aware of movement and looked up. Harriet was standing in the window. Lynam could not see her face, but could tell from her back that she was crying. When the effect of this soundless anguish became too much Lynam went to the lavatory. She stood staring blankly at the Delft bowl with its throne-like mahogany seating. She was there quite a while, teeth and fists clenched against the rigours of trembling when the door creaked open. Gallagher. She recognised his jeans and desert boots. She did not look up and felt nothing. When he said without inflection, 'You all right Lynam?' she kicked the door shut with both feet. Gradually she began to feel normal, blood running in arteries and with it warmth returning.

As she returned to the room only the McAleers smiled. She sat separately watching the afternoon shadow edge across the wide bleached floorboards in the bay window. The silence and purity of light, and the tension of stillness became so oppressive that she stood. As she did, a megaphoned voice bombarded the house:

'A word requested with Colonel Armstrong at the front door.'

She saw Leonard nod immediately at the Colonel. She went to the window. Standing behind Leonard she could see out and down. With a dull nausea she saw what had distressed Harriet; Boyd-Crawford curled in the grass, an abandoned foetus wrapped in tweed and hessian. The officer said about three sentences. As the Colonel came back, Leonard went to meet him.

Lynam watched them walk to the other end of the hall. Twice they paused, neither looking at the other. The Colonel then moved away and stood looking up through the banisters at an Italian landscape hanging on the panelled wall of the wide, slow-raked stairs, waiting. For what seemed like minutes Leonard stood rooted, staring at centuries of wear on the flagged floor. Was he going to consult? It was clear that what had been suggested or threatened was unexpected. He glanced up, caught her unmoving eyes and almost immediately looked away and approached the Colonel. From the way they spoke, turned about, and listened intently, she had no doubt that some form of compromise had been agreed. She could sense Gallagher alongside her, alert, listening. Without looking at him she said:

'Can you hear?'

'He knows what he's at.'

'Do you?'

There was quite a pause before Gallagher asked:

'Do I what?'

'Know what he's at?'

'We don't matter.'

An acid comment occurred. She let it go. No time left now for anything but the pervasive and increasing fear. What was agreed?

She had heard, or imagined she had heard, the word 'disarming' and saw Leonard nod. She stood back now as they crossed the hall, the Colonel in front. She kept looking in Leonard's face. Again she got the impression that he deliberately avoided her eyes. He said as he followed the Colonel into the room: 'They're bringing them.'

The McAleers laughed.

'Powerful.'

'Good man Martin.'

'He was right all along.'

'He always is.'

Gallagher smiled watchfully. Lynam's expression like Gallagher's was questioning. There was no triumph in Leonard's voice as he announced the release, and he seemed even bleaker as he said:

'I might take a drink now.'

The Colonel poured. Leonard took the whiskey, walked away and stood by himself at the fireplace. As Gallagher moved towards him Leonard said with sudden sharpness:

'Keep watch all of you.'

Gallagher kept looking at Leonard with a suspicion verging on menace. With reluctance he went back as ordered to the doorway. They took up their positions again. Lynam could not catch Leonard's eye. After five minutes she came over to him.

'They're bringing them?'

'Yes.'

'When?'

'Soon. An hour, maybe less.'

'Why did they wait till now? . . . So stupid . . . '

Leonard shrugged.

'It's a trick,' she said.

'If it is, we go ahead as planned.'

Both Harriet and Canon Plumm were questioning the Colonel with their eyes. He would not be drawn other than saying:

'I think it's all right.'

'Thank God,' Canon Plumm said.

Leonard finished his whiskey and poured another. He had made up his mind, but the more he thought about it, the more doubtful he became as he visualised its execution. For three years his life had been one unnerving choice. He had grown accustomed to hard decisions, but this one involved very cold thinking. The killing of the first victim compromised his position. He left his second whiskey untouched on the mantel beside the clock: 12.30. The helicopter, unless they planned shock action in the meantime, should arrive at 2. He felt suddenly very tired. He went to the couch and lay down and closed his eyes. An hour passed. Then he heard Gallagher's voice at his ear.

'The snag, Martin.'

He looked at Gallagher. There was no way of lying to that cold ungiving face, always a move ahead.

'We'll have to wait.'

'The snag?'

'We must wait.'

'You're lying.'

'Tired.'

'Not that kind.'

'Careful Jack.'

'They don't do things that way, I want to know.'

Leonard looked at Lynam. He knew that, like Gallagher, she could sense something unforeseen, unexpected. There was no way he could tell them.

'I won't be pushed Jack.'

When Gallagher accepted that Leonard would not be forced to speak he began to move. Leonard watched him obey then gave a silent whistle. Gallagher came back and bent towards Leonard who whispered. Gallagher straightened. For quite a while he stood thinking. Finally he nodded and glanced at Lynam with a look almost akin to compassion. As she saw this look a feeling of doom crept about her heart. What had been said? Was Gallagher privy to it? If so why was she excluded:

'There was a deal,' she said.

Leonard nodded.

'What?'

'Presently.'

The Colonel looked up from a book called *Beautiful Flowering Shrubs*, by G. Clarke Nuttal, opened at chapter XVIII, 'The Evergreen Rhododendrons'.

He had read the same paragraph three times without comprehension. He now turned the pages looking at splendid colour illustrations. Now and then he showed a plate to his wife who nodded and said: 'Exquisite' or 'Beautiful'. Canon Plumm continued with the *Selected Sunday Readings*. Now and then he pointed out a passage to Harriet who read, smoking continuously.

At ten past two they all heard the helicopter approaching. As it dropped to silence Leonard got up, nodding towards the Colonel. In the hall Leonard said:

'If they're here we take two of you as far as the helicopter.'

'Disarming?'

'When you come back.'

The Colonel went down behind the armoured wagons

and was back in less than a minute. As he came in the door he said to Leonard:

'They're here.'

Leonard went into the room and walked towards Lynam. He picked up her handbag, took out the pistol and put it in his back pocket. Baffled, half understanding, she watched as he approached Pascal and whispered. Pascal handed his pistol to Leonard. He then approached Pacelli, who also handed him his pistol. Leonard then handed one of the pistols to Gallagher.

'What are you doing?' Lynam asked.

Leonard did not reply. He walked to the Adam fireplace and stood under the great gilt mirror. Gallagher moved from the window towards the far end of the room and stood where everyone was well in focus. Leonard had obviously prepared and picked his words with great care, speaking now in such a low voice that all had to strain to catch what he said.

'The offer was nothing or . . . three for three . . . ' He paused. 'The men being released you know about . . . their value . . . I had to choose . . . I've chosen.'

Lynam listened unbelieving as the spare words branded her accessory to murder, condemned her to the brutality and living death of a prison compound. Leonard was looking at Pascal and Pacelli as he said:

'I'm sorry boys . . . Your mother will be cared.'

He turned to Lynam. What he had intended saying now seemed inadequate. Suddenly behind those hooded eyes she saw meanness, cowardice and treachery. Before he could speak she said:

'Picked yourself! . . . My God you're a coward.'

She was on her feet, trembling so much she could scarcely speak. She nodded at Gallagher.

'Picked . . . him . . . before me?'

'He does what he does better than you.'

He stopped himself from adding: 'And so do they.'

Her voice was shrill as she said: 'Psychopathic and you know it.'

'Then so am I . . . I won't judge and I've decided . . . I'm sorry.'

'You're not . . . The captain and the first mate leaving the crew to sink; they'll write ballads about you Commandant when you're court-martialled . . . Coward and Leonard will rhyme well enough.'

The words stung. What she said now had occurred to Leonard again and again in the two hour wait. He was certain that Burke and the military council would approve but regret his decision. Two bomb technicians and a suspect propagandist were nothing like the force, drive and dedication of the three men released. And he had to decide that Gallagher and himself were the most useful of the five. Enemies would whisper what she had just called him now, the only word that shames a soldier. The fact that he had killed before witnesses and cameras excluded the possibility of a chivalrous offer to stay. If one of the brothers had killed he would have chosen him to go. One way or another Lynam would have been left. Gallagher's voice came from the corner.

'This is not a cruise where captains drown with honour, it's war; he commands . . . you obey . . . that's it.' Less harshly he said: 'If you prize your life that much, you go, I'll stay. That goes for the boys too.'

Leonard was about to intervene when Pascal and Pacelli said simultaneously:

'I'll go by Martin.'

'Me too, Martin's right.'

Gallagher asked:

'Well?'

'You mean it?'

'I mean it.'

Were nice guys bastards, and bastards noble? Still unbelieving she looked from Leonard to Gallagher. Was he bluffing? She had only to say yes. As she looked she realised that Gallagher's offer was contemptuous. He was flaunting his prowess as a killer against her troubled conscience and humanity. Far from Carton country he was turning the screw with cruel psychological cunning, daring her to choose herself before him. To accept his offer would be vastly more ignominious than the grim, fast-looming alternative. She felt now that every word, step, and sequence had led inevitably to this moment of terror and rejection. Very quietly she said:

'I prefer gaol to either of you.'

'That,' Gallagher said, 'is no surprise.'

There was a noise of footsteps on gravel. Leonard went to the side of the bay window: Caldwell again on his way to the house. To the Colonel, Leonard said:

'We take you and the Canon.'

Gallagher embraced both Pascal and Pacelli. From where he stood he directed his voice towards Lynam and said:

'Slán.'

She did not answer.

When Leonard had shaken hands with the brothers he looked at Lynam. As he approached her she said:

'His offer was an insult . . . I'd rather be dead than see you rule.'

Leonard thought his thoughts. He did not express them. With his unaltering voice he said:

'I know.'

As he turned to go, Gallagher took him aside. Sensing what he would say Leonard said: 'She didn't mean that.'

'She said it . . . all she knows Martin . . . who, why, when, what . . . they'll get it . . . we can't leave her!'

'The offer is three for three.'

As Gallagher pondered the reality Leonard said: 'I've had two hours to think: this is the only way.'

'I'll stay for one of the boys.'

'You'll not.'

'I want to Martin.'

'Bomb technicians are two a penny . . . you're needed.'

'We're soldiers . . . we should . . . we can't leave them, Martin . . . not both.'

'When I move, move with me; ready?'

For ten seconds it seemed to Leonard that Gallagher would not obey. Without looking at him he asked again: 'Ready?'

'Ready,' Gallagher said.

Leonard motioned the Colonel and Canon Plumm to the hall. Gallagher made a pushing away movement with his free hand towards the brothers, a gesture of defeat and farewell. In response the McAleers stood and saluted. Leonard acknowledged the salute bleakly and followed. As they went Lynam sat lost, her back to the window. Gradually she became aware first of Harriet's eyes, then voice saying:

'*A tale lamentable of things ill done*
For the Living Dead: no comfort from the sun.'

As Harriet left the room Pascal and Pacelli approached, both smiling unnaturally. She stared into their faces.

'They'll brutalise . . . torture us.'

'Don't think on it, love,' Pascal said.

'Bounce of the ball,' Pacelli added.

'Some must suffer.'

'We'll laugh five years from now.'

'Aye to be sure.'

'Show them you're not afeered Bella.'

'Stand, you're a soldier.'

'Put on bravery . . . face them with us.'

As she stood between them they kissed her as they had kissed her the evening before.

Harriet watched from the door as three camera crews filmed th four walking across the front of the Tudor house towards the waiting helicopter. When they were out of sight she went to Alex, knelt at hs head and uncovered the face. The two bullets had entered his skull within the hairline leaving his face unmarked. She pulled off her shoe and propped it under his chin to close his mouth, shutting his eyes with her thumbs, aware of soldiers running across the gravel towards the steps. They ran past her into the house. Then a British officer was beside her on one knee holding her arm:

'Mrs Armstrong.'

'Yes.'

'We'll attend to that.'

'I can manage . . . a friend . . . a dear, dear friend, so kind, a human being, do you understand?'

'Of course.'

'A human being.'

She shook her head. Alex's face blurred.

'I think you should come inside.'

The officer was exerting gentle pressure on her arm.

'No . . . I . . . perfectly all right.'

From her knees she saw the McAleers and Lynam come through the front door escorted by soldiers. As Lynam slowed to say something she was pushed roughly onwards by soldiers. Harriet bowed her head and wept. The helicopter rose from the side of the house, its blade whirling in the afternoon sun, a monstrous insect heading south across the quiet lake, meadow and forest.

When she looked up, the Colonel and the Canon

were being interviewed by television reporters. Caldwell stood behind the camera crews watching. A reporter and a camera man with a hand-held camera approached the steps. The officer stood up and waved them away. They kept coming and he said:

'Please gentlemen, please . . . later.'

Harriet saw them coming, stood and said: 'I don't mind, provided they don't show Alex like that.'

They were three yards away now. The camera began to whirr.

'What do you want to know? Surely it's clear!'

The reporter said: 'I understand you were brutally beaten Mrs Armstrong.'

Harriet shook her head.

'Your face is bruised.'

'Nothing.'

'What is your feeling now?'

'My feeling? . . . about what?'

The reporter hesitated, unsure. She waited till he asked: 'A few minutes ago you were at death's door.'

Harriet nodded. 'Yes . . . well . . . my feeling.'

She paused, apparently unable to go on. The officer shook his head motioning the reporter to cut the interview.

'No, no I can answer . . . my feeling at the moment is one of . . . desolation . . . of unutterable despair . . . that is my feeling now . . . despair . . . but look around you.'

Harriet looked out over the massive shapes of war and the uniforms below, to the long lake, the great forest beyond and up into the August sun, the blinding sky.

'Look about you.'

Her face fell apart as she said: 'The world is still beautiful.'

She nodded trying to smile and said again:

'Beautiful.'

A Selected List of Titles Available from Minerva